Howard Pyle's

Robin Hood

Adapted by
Joe Dunn

Illustrated by
Ben Dunn

magic
Wagon

visit us at
www.abdopublishing.com

Published by Magic Wagon, a division of the ABDO Publishing Group, 8000 West 78th Street, Edina, Minnesota 55439.

Printed in the United States.

Original novel by Howard Pyle
Adapted by Joe Dunn
Illustrated by Ben Dunn
Colored by Robby Bevard
Lettered by Joe Dunn
Edited by Stephanie Hedlund
Interior layout and design by Antarctic Press
Cover art by Ben Dunn
Cover design by Neil Klinepier

Library of Congress Cataloging-in-Publication Data

Dunn, Joeming W.
Robin Hood / Howard Pyle ; adapted by Joe Dunn ; illustrated by Ben Dunn.
p. cm. -- (Graphic classics)
Includes bibliographical references.
ISBN 978-1-60270-053-6
1. Graphic novels. I. Dunn, Ben. II. Pyle, Howard, 1853-1911. Merry Adventures of Robin Hood. III. Title.

PN6727.D89R63 2008
741.5'973--dc22

2007006445

TABLE of CONTENTS

Chapter 1
Nottingham..4

Chapter 2
The Merry Men...10

Chapter 3
Training the Men...13

Chapter 4
Maid Marian...18

Chapter 5
The Games Begin..22

Chapter 6
The King Returns..27

About the Author...30

Additional Works...31

About the Adapter..31

Glossary...32

Web Sites...32

Chapter 1 Nottingham

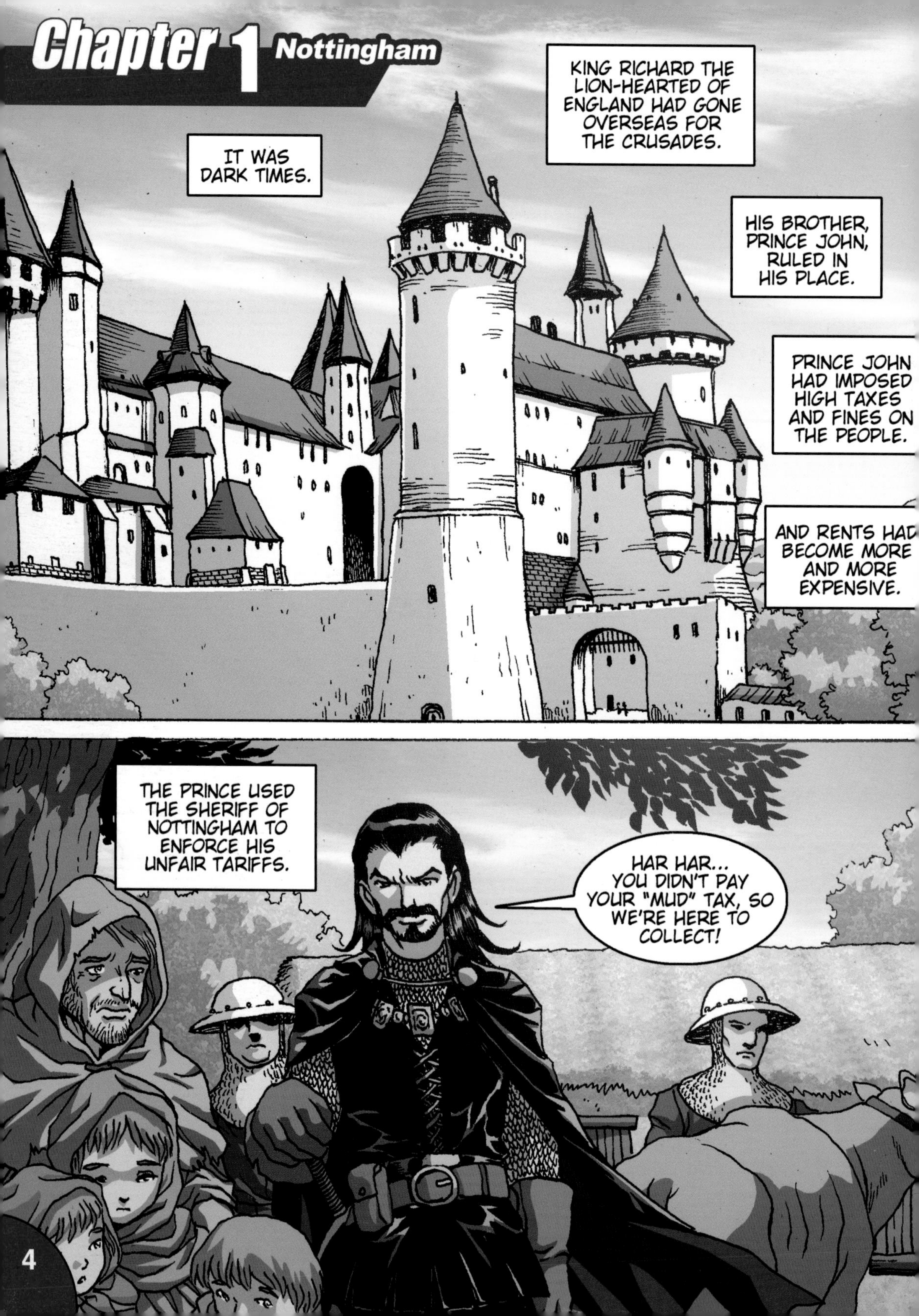
IT WAS DARK TIMES.
KING RICHARD THE LION-HEARTED OF ENGLAND HAD GONE OVERSEAS FOR THE CRUSADES.
HIS BROTHER, PRINCE JOHN, RULED IN HIS PLACE.
PRINCE JOHN HAD IMPOSED HIGH TAXES AND FINES ON THE PEOPLE.
AND RENTS HAD BECOME MORE AND MORE EXPENSIVE.
THE PRINCE USED THE SHERIFF OF NOTTINGHAM TO ENFORCE HIS UNFAIR TARIFFS.
HAR HAR... YOU DIDN'T PAY YOUR "MUD" TAX, SO WE'RE HERE TO COLLECT!

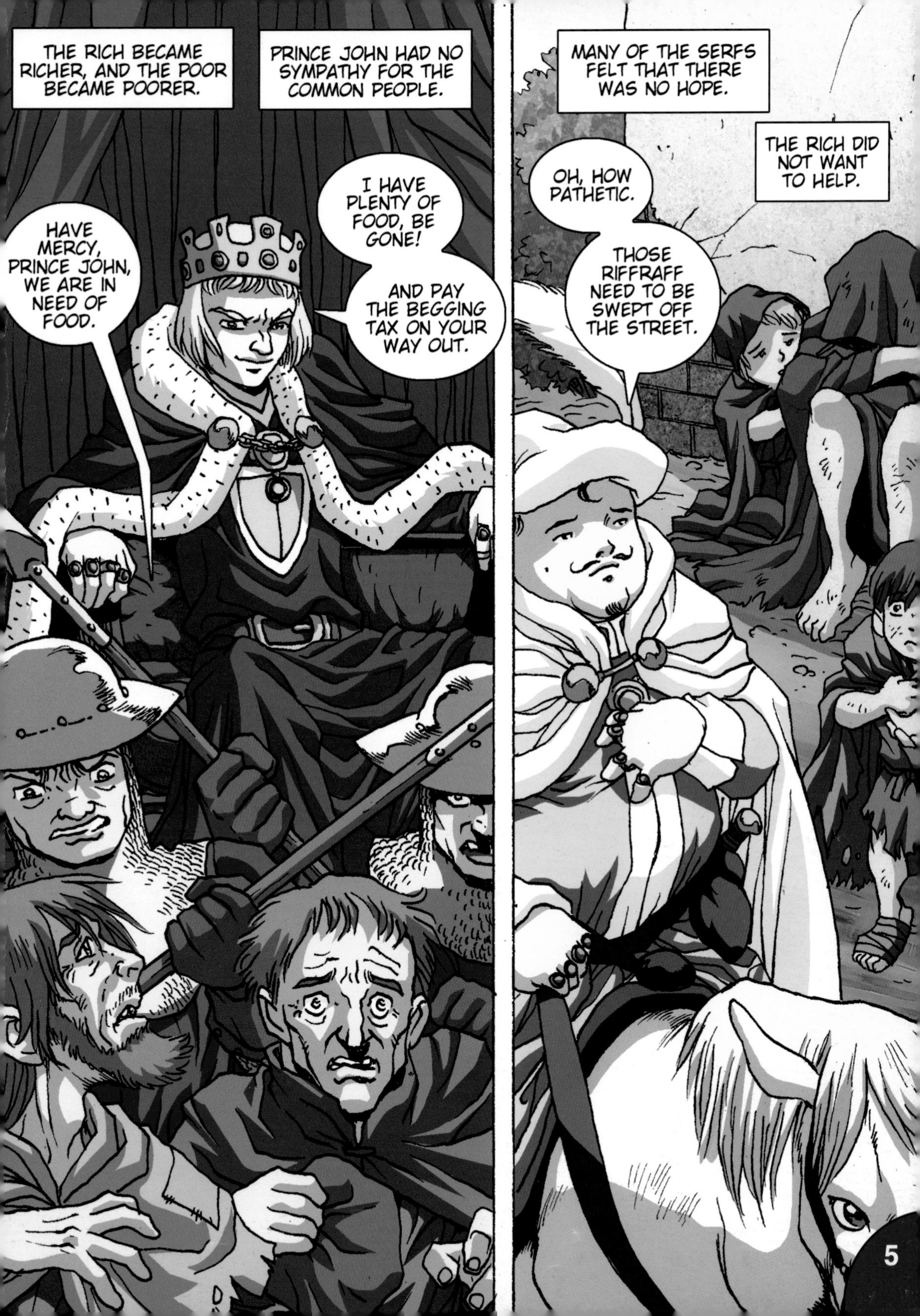
THE RICH BECAME RICHER, AND THE POOR BECAME POORER.
PRINCE JOHN HAD NO SYMPATHY FOR THE COMMON PEOPLE.
HAVE MERCY, PRINCE JOHN, WE ARE IN NEED OF FOOD.
I HAVE PLENTY OF FOOD, BE GONE!
AND PAY THE BEGGING TAX ON YOUR WAY OUT.
MANY OF THE SERFS FELT THAT THERE WAS NO HOPE.
THE RICH DID NOT WANT TO HELP.
OH, HOW PATHETIC.
THOSE RIFFRAFF NEED TO BE SWEPT OFF THE STREET.

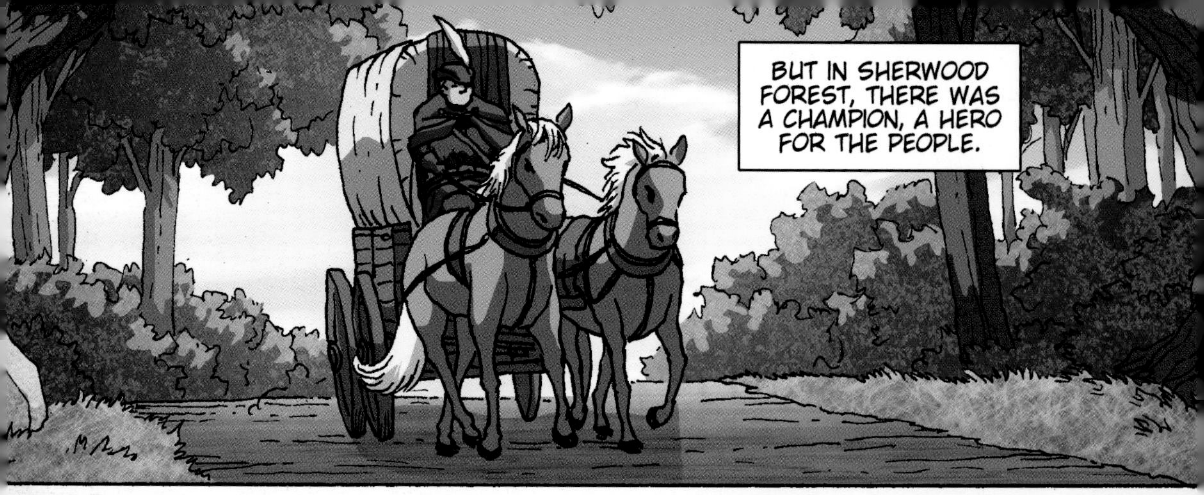
BUT IN SHERWOOD FOREST, THERE WAS A CHAMPION, A HERO FOR THE PEOPLE.

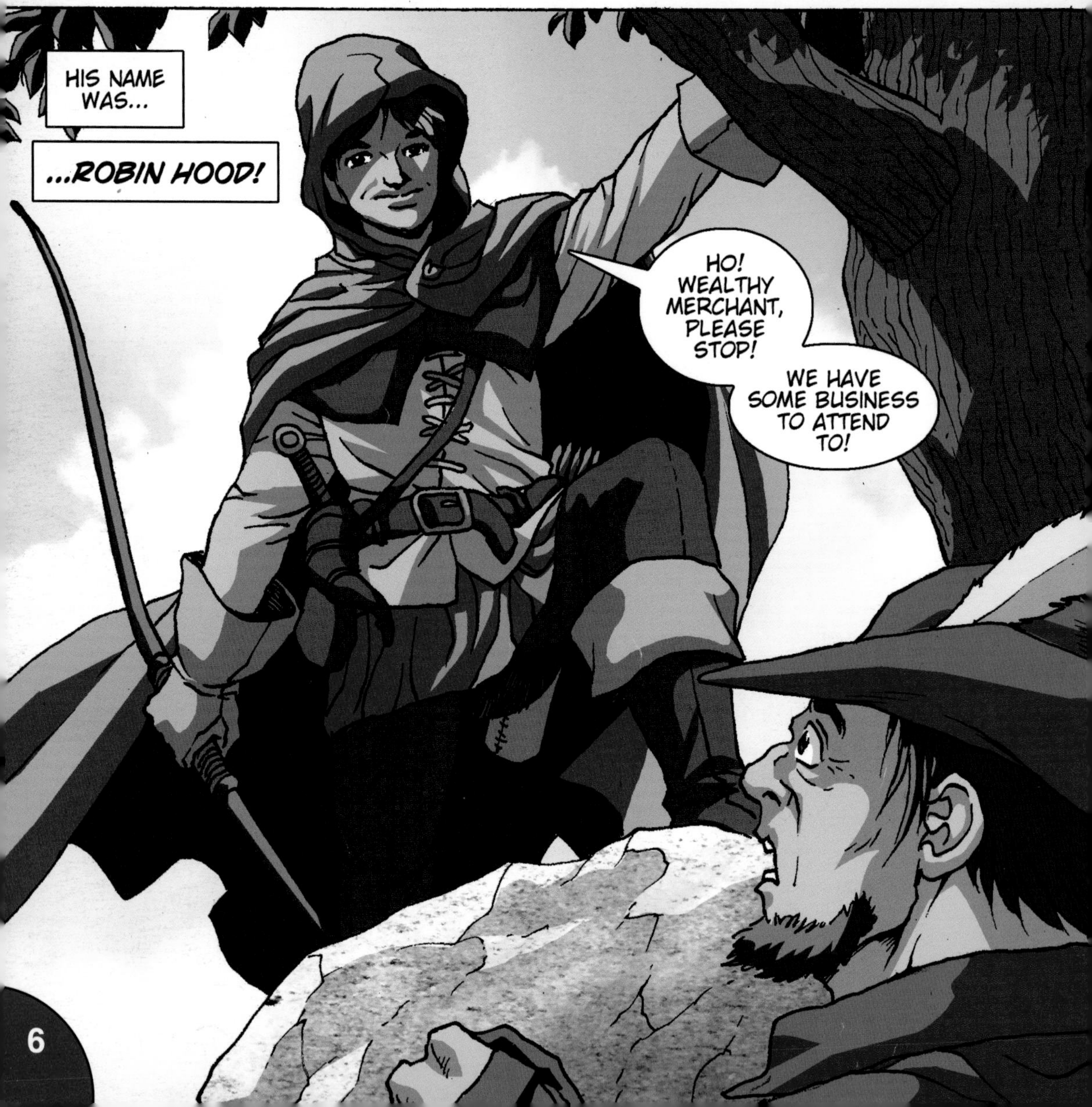
HIS NAME WAS...
...ROBIN HOOD!
HO! WEALTHY MERCHANT, PLEASE STOP!
WE HAVE SOME BUSINESS TO ATTEND TO!

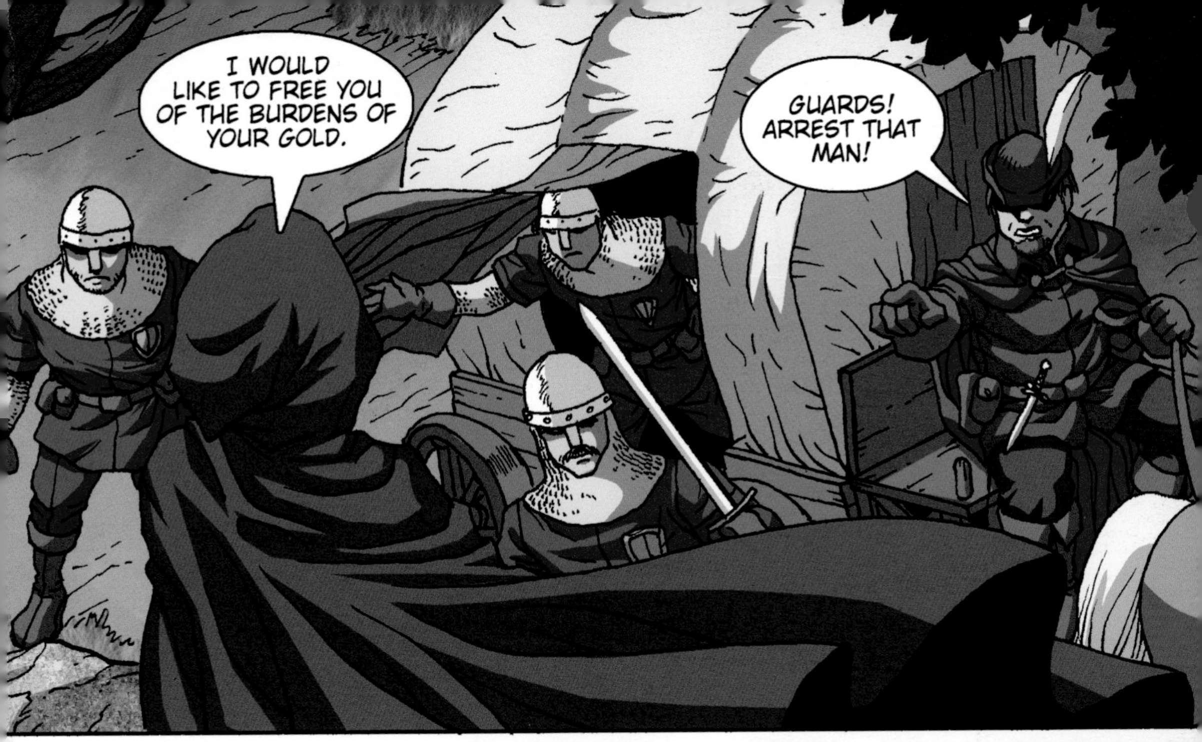
I WOULD LIKE TO FREE YOU OF THE BURDENS OF YOUR GOLD.
GUARDS! ARREST THAT MAN!

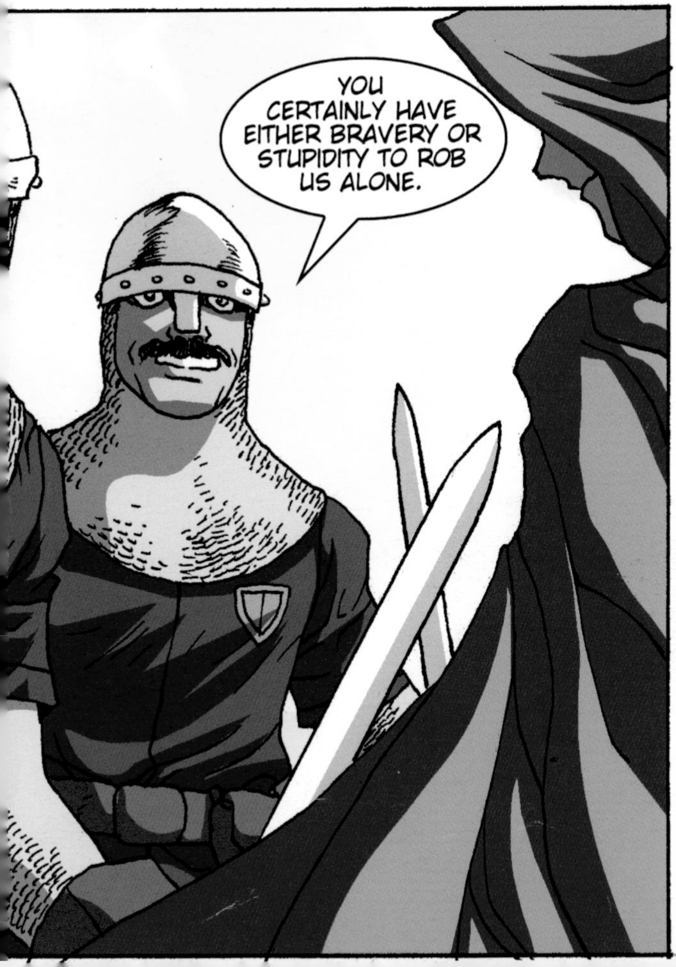
YOU CERTAINLY HAVE EITHER BRAVERY OR STUPIDITY TO ROB US ALONE.

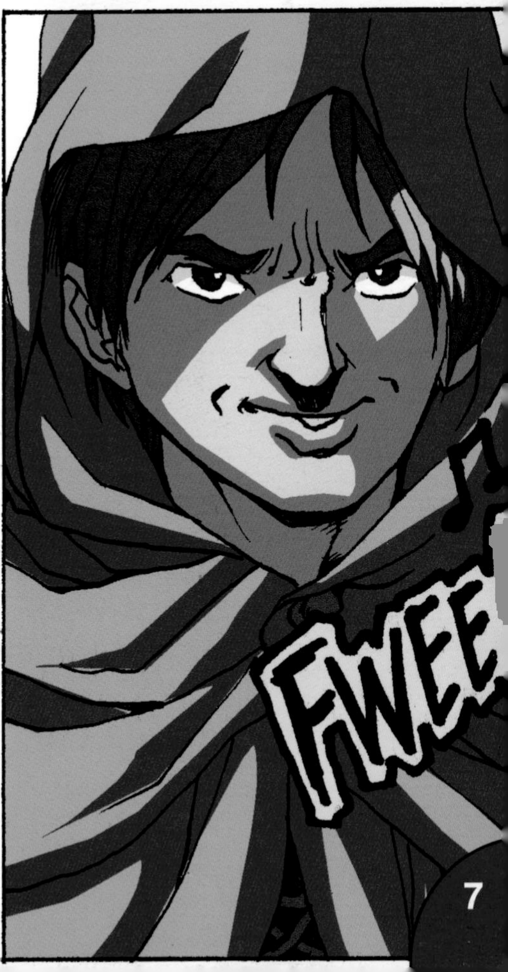
FWEE

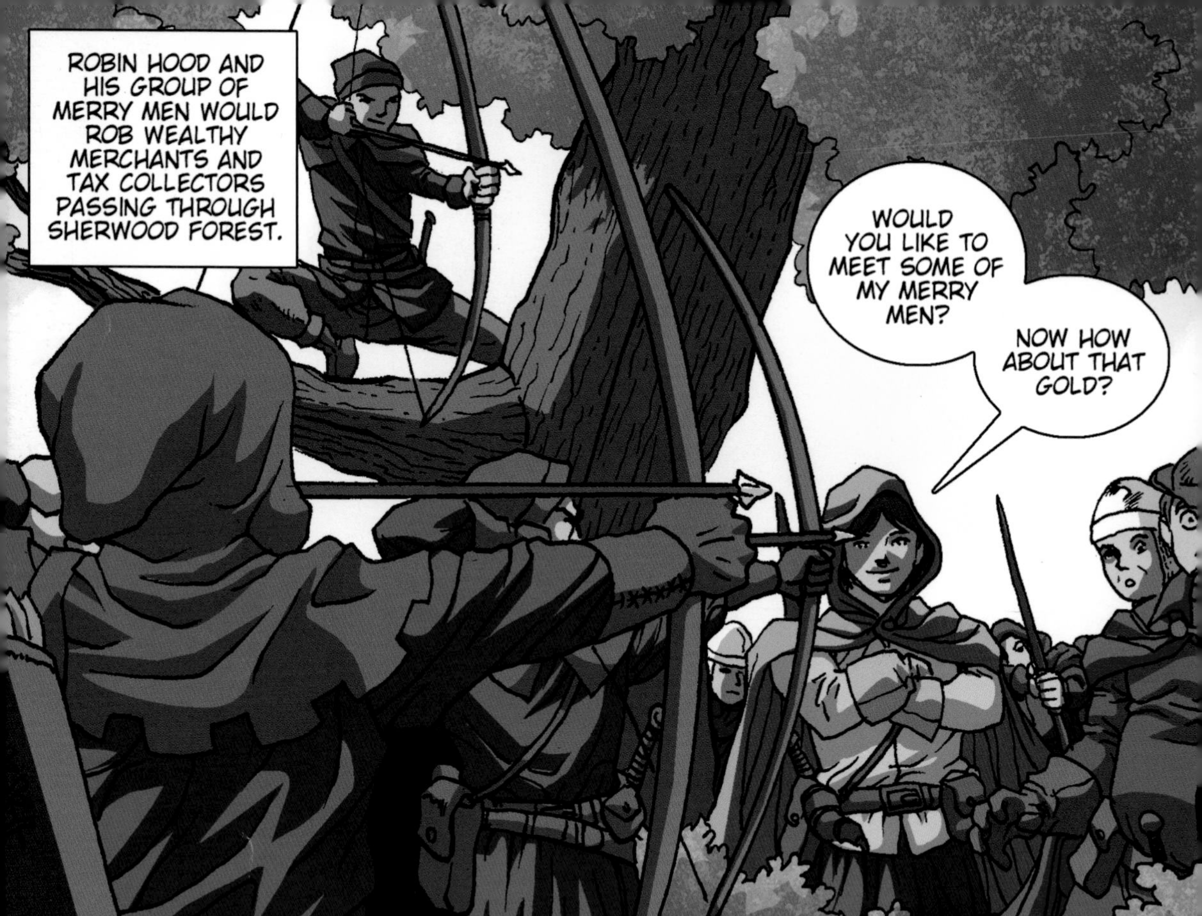
ROBIN HOOD AND HIS GROUP OF MERRY MEN WOULD ROB WEALTHY MERCHANTS AND TAX COLLECTORS PASSING THROUGH SHERWOOD FOREST.
WOULD YOU LIKE TO MEET SOME OF MY MERRY MEN?
NOW HOW ABOUT THAT GOLD?

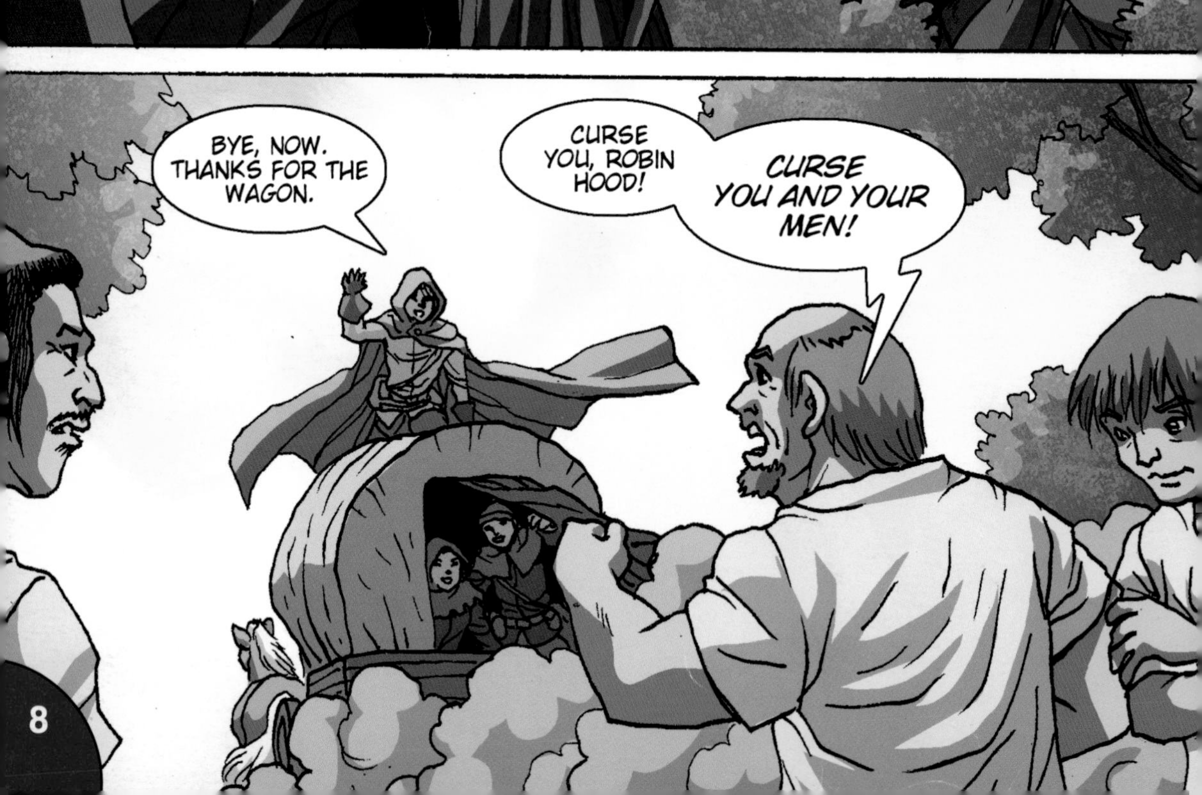
BYE, NOW. THANKS FOR THE WAGON.
CURSE YOU, ROBIN HOOD!
CURSE YOU AND YOUR MEN!

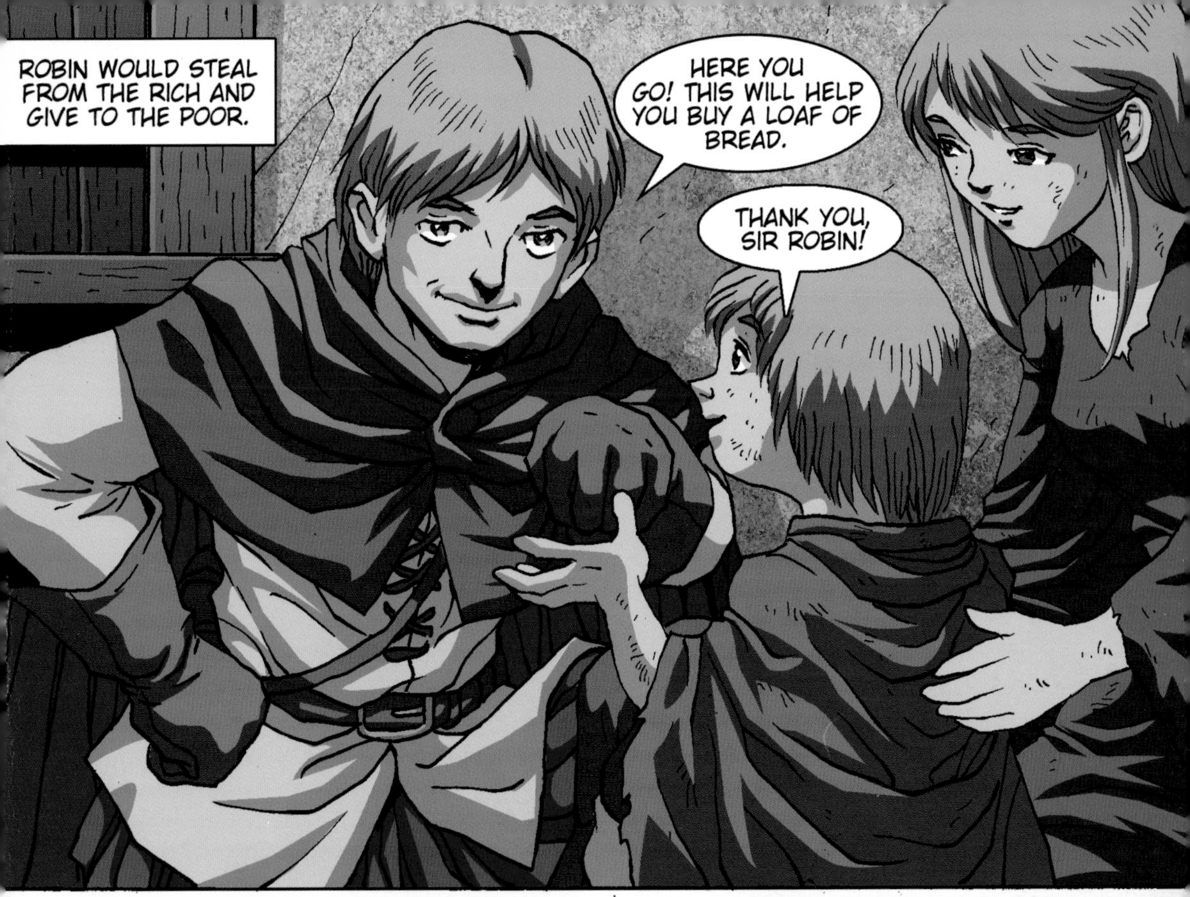
ROBIN WOULD STEAL FROM THE RICH AND GIVE TO THE POOR.
HERE YOU GO! THIS WILL HELP YOU BUY A LOAF OF BREAD.
THANK YOU, SIR ROBIN!

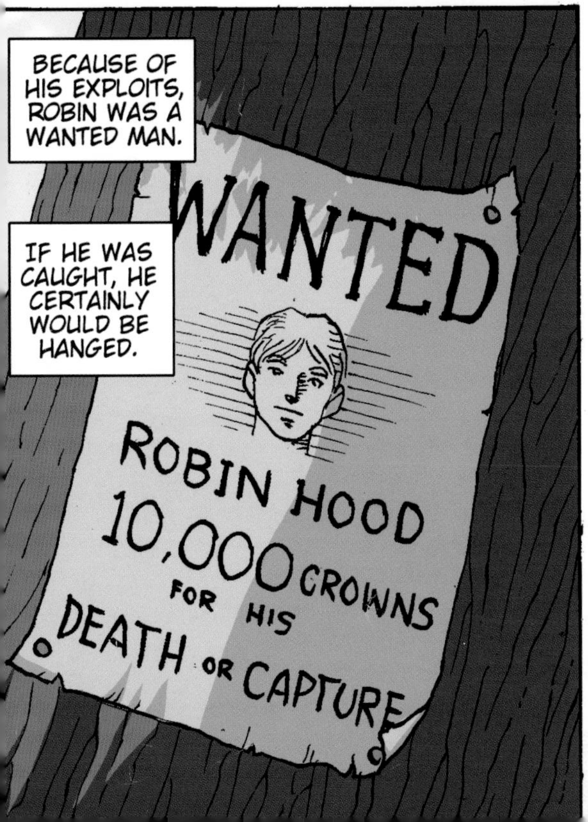
BECAUSE OF HIS EXPLOITS, ROBIN WAS A WANTED MAN.
IF HE WAS CAUGHT, HE CERTAINLY WOULD BE HANGED.
WANTED
ROBIN HOOD
10,000 CROWNS
FOR HIS
DEATH OR CAPTURE

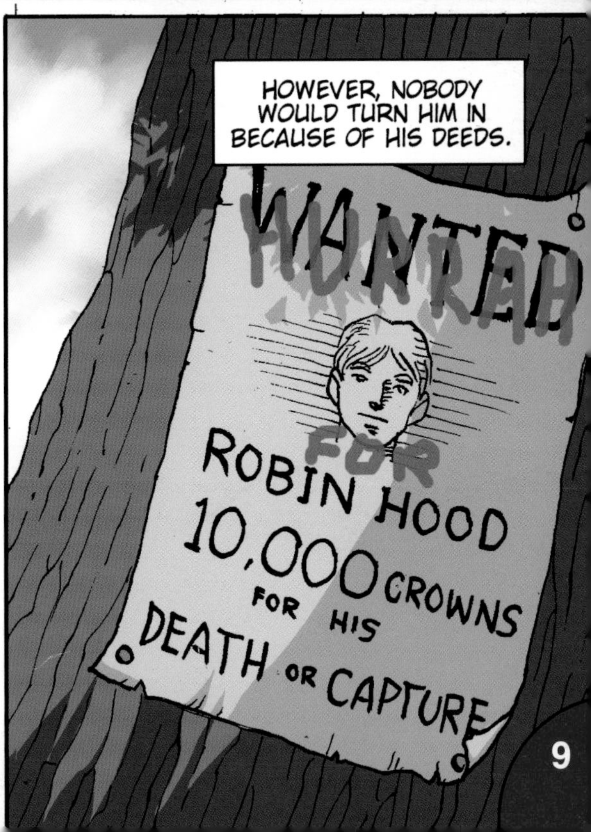
HOWEVER, NOBODY WOULD TURN HIM IN BECAUSE OF HIS DEEDS.
WANTED
HURRAH
FOR
ROBIN HOOD
10,000 CROWNS
FOR HIS
DEATH OR CAPTURE

Chapter 2 The Merry Men

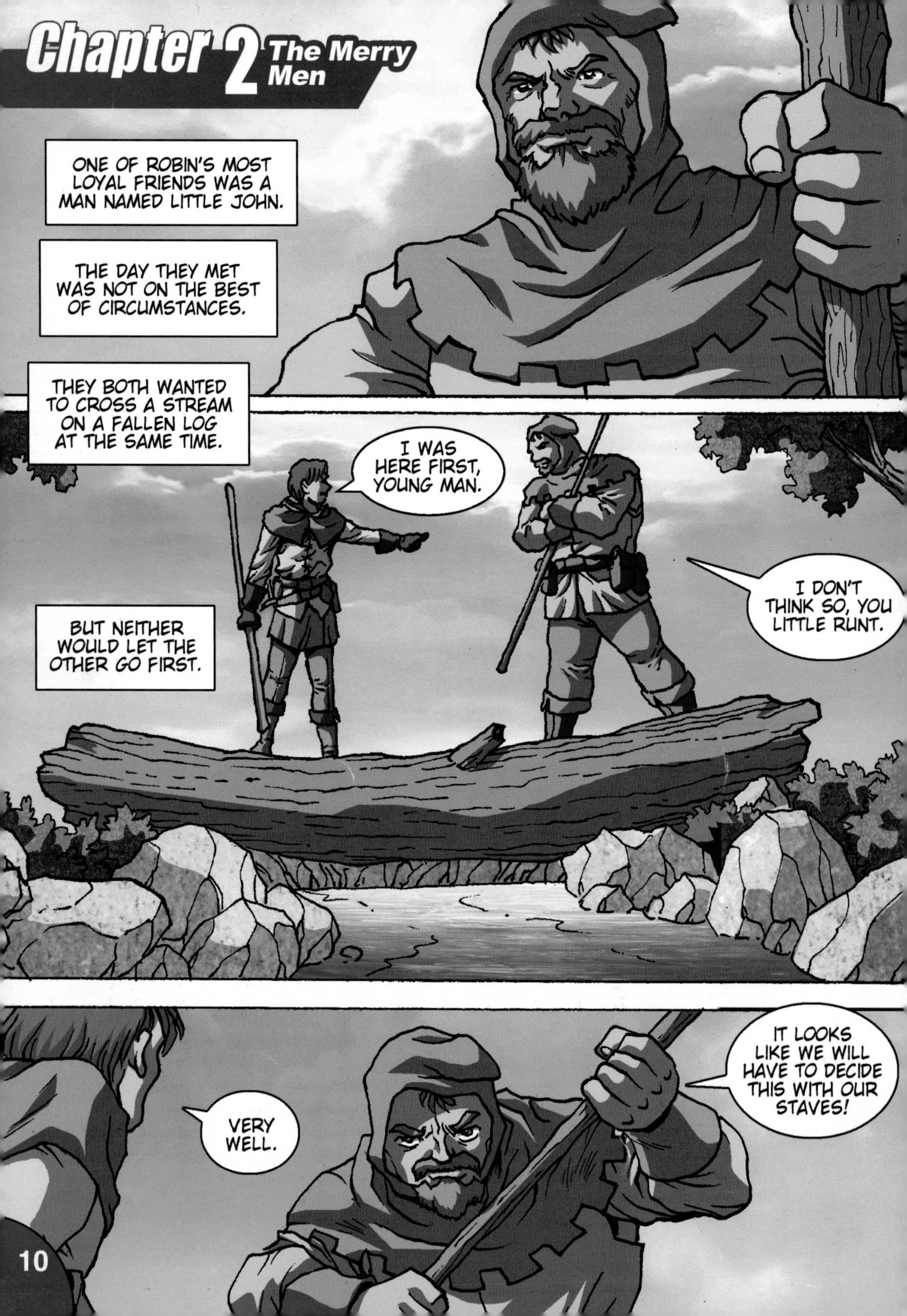
ONE OF ROBIN'S MOST LOYAL FRIENDS WAS A MAN NAMED LITTLE JOHN.
THE DAY THEY MET WAS NOT ON THE BEST OF CIRCUMSTANCES.
THEY BOTH WANTED TO CROSS A STREAM ON A FALLEN LOG AT THE SAME TIME.
I WAS HERE FIRST, YOUNG MAN.
I DON'T THINK SO, YOU LITTLE RUNT.
BUT NEITHER WOULD LET THE OTHER GO FIRST.
IT LOOKS LIKE WE WILL HAVE TO DECIDE THIS WITH OUR STAVES!
VERY WELL.

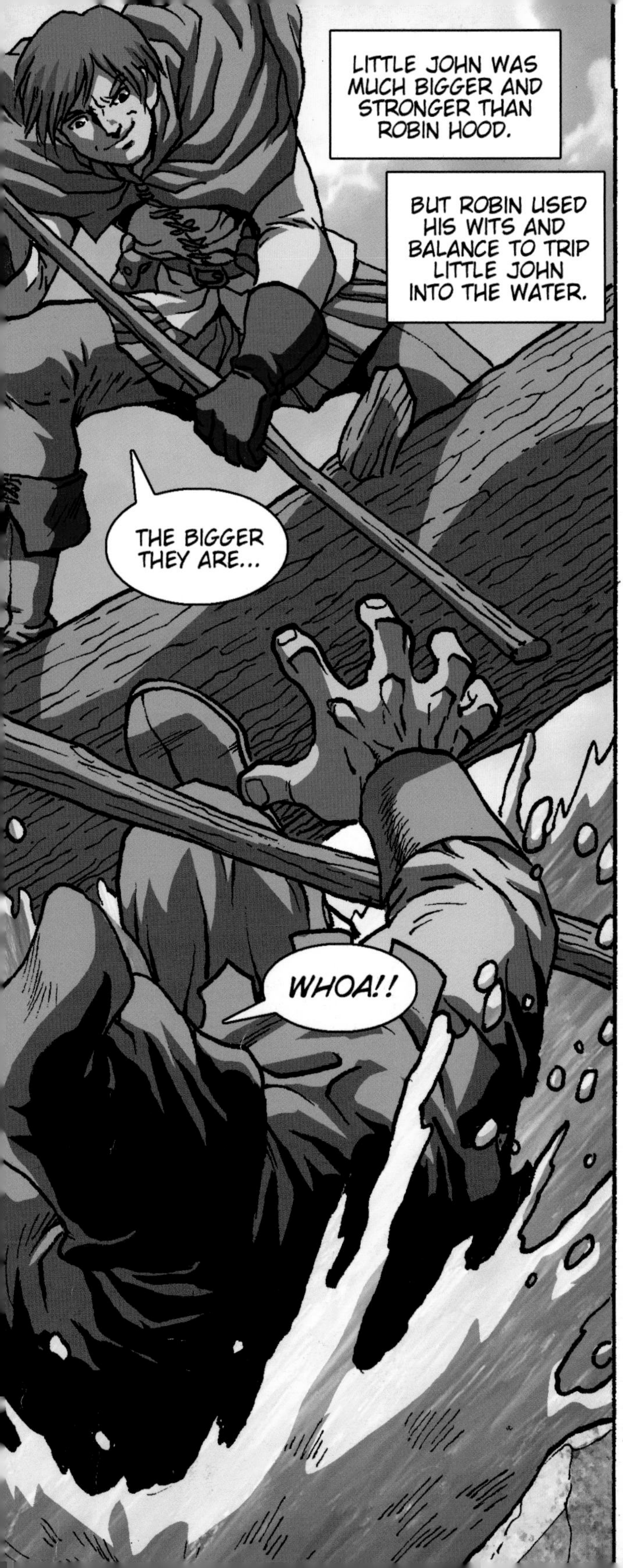
LITTLE JOHN WAS MUCH BIGGER AND STRONGER THAN ROBIN HOOD.
BUT ROBIN USED HIS WITS AND BALANCE TO TRIP LITTLE JOHN INTO THE WATER.
THE BIGGER THEY ARE...
WHOA!!

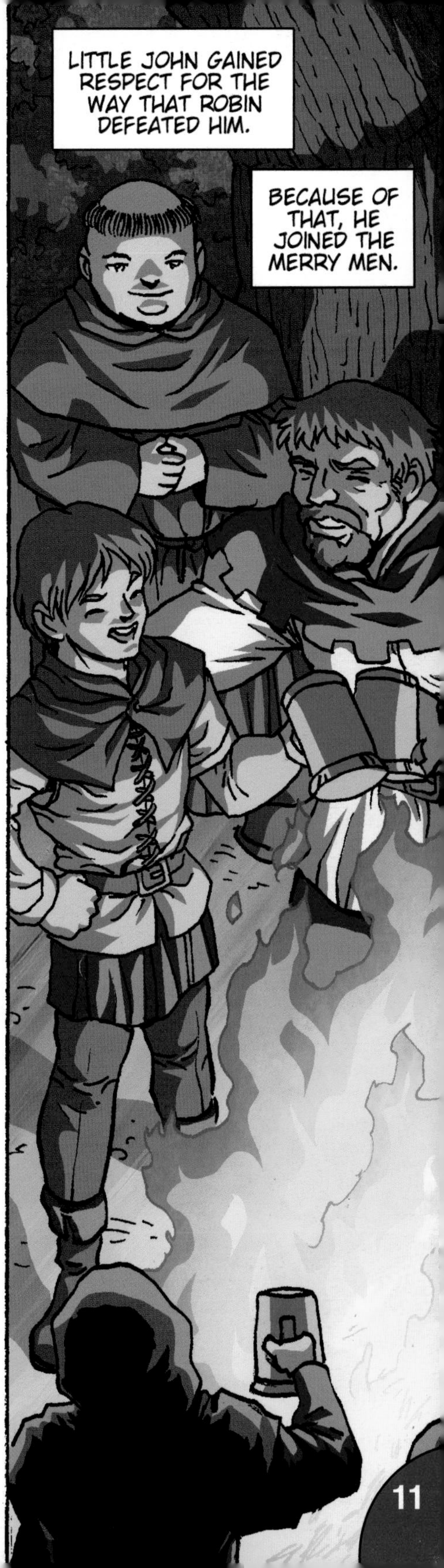
LITTLE JOHN GAINED RESPECT FOR THE WAY THAT ROBIN DEFEATED HIM.
BECAUSE OF THAT, HE JOINED THE MERRY MEN.

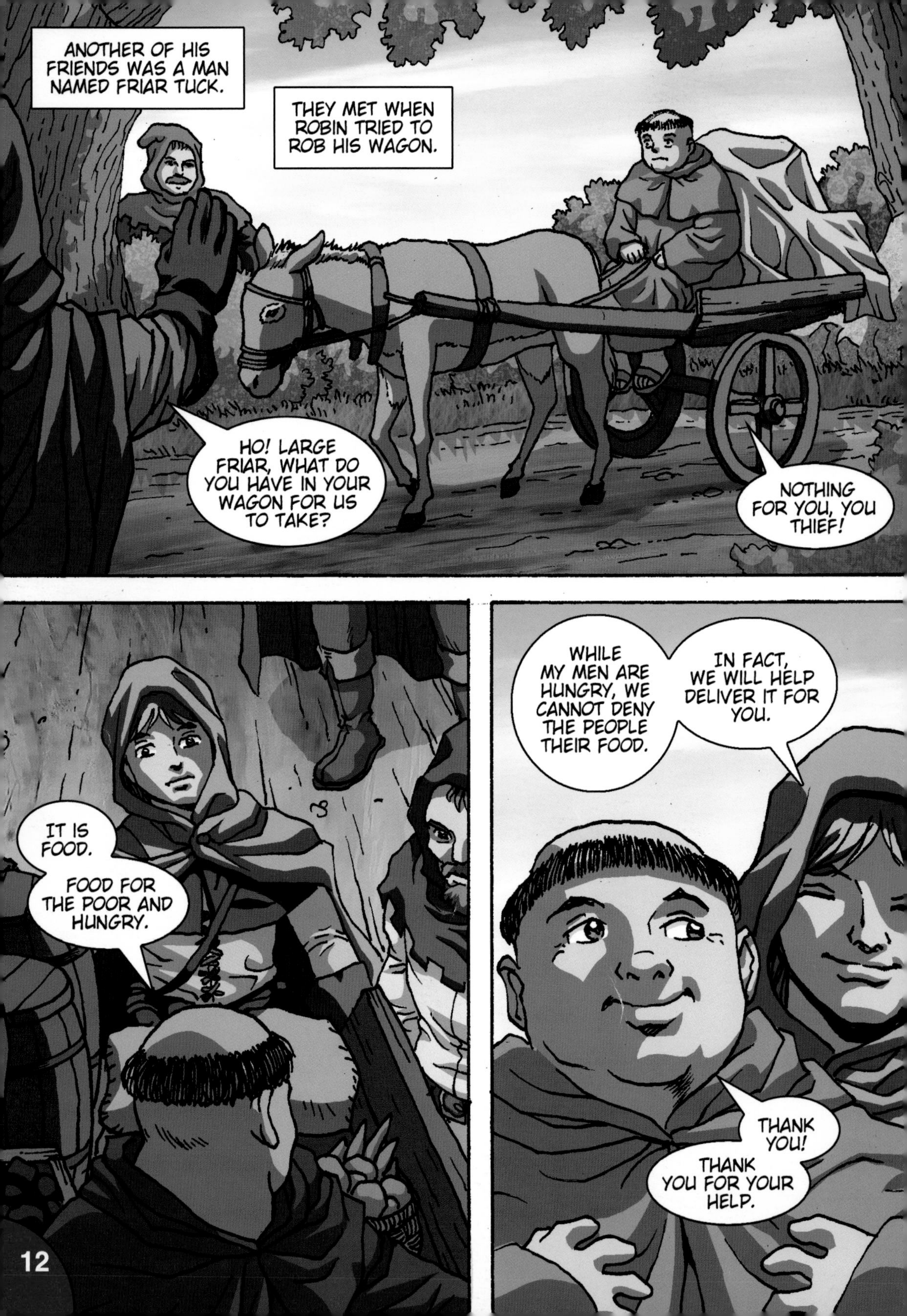

ANOTHER OF HIS FRIENDS WAS A MAN NAMED FRIAR TUCK.
THEY MET WHEN ROBIN TRIED TO ROB HIS WAGON.
HO! LARGE FRIAR, WHAT DO YOU HAVE IN YOUR WAGON FOR US TO TAKE?
NOTHING FOR YOU, YOU THIEF!
IT IS FOOD.
FOOD FOR THE POOR AND HUNGRY.
WHILE MY MEN ARE HUNGRY, WE CANNOT DENY THE PEOPLE THEIR FOOD.
IN FACT, WE WILL HELP DELIVER IT FOR YOU.
THANK YOU!
THANK YOU FOR YOUR HELP.

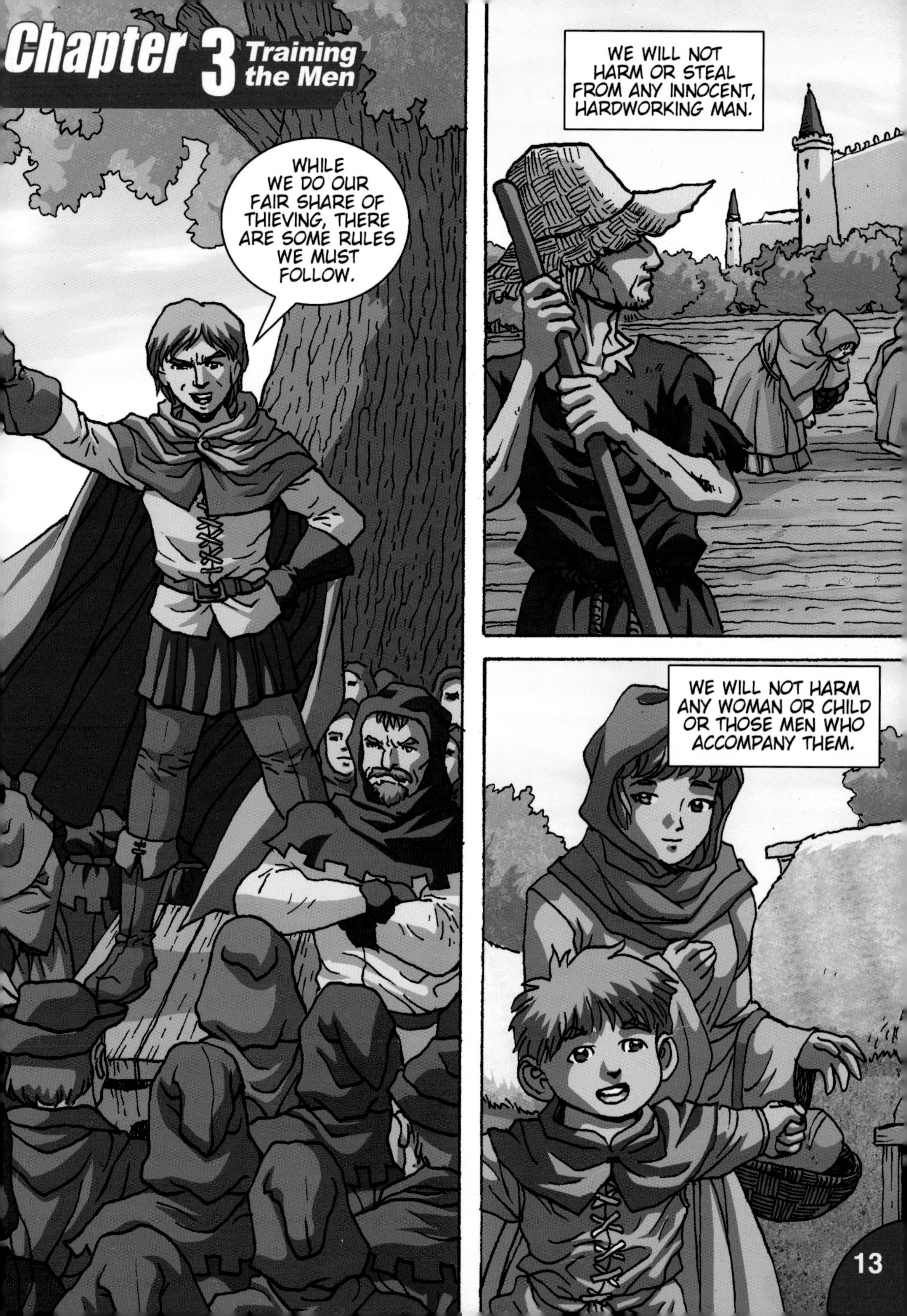
Chapter 3 Training the Men
WHILE WE DO OUR FAIR SHARE OF THIEVING, THERE ARE SOME RULES WE MUST FOLLOW.
WE WILL NOT HARM OR STEAL FROM ANY INNOCENT, HARDWORKING MAN.
WE WILL NOT HARM ANY WOMAN OR CHILD OR THOSE MEN WHO ACCOMPANY THEM.

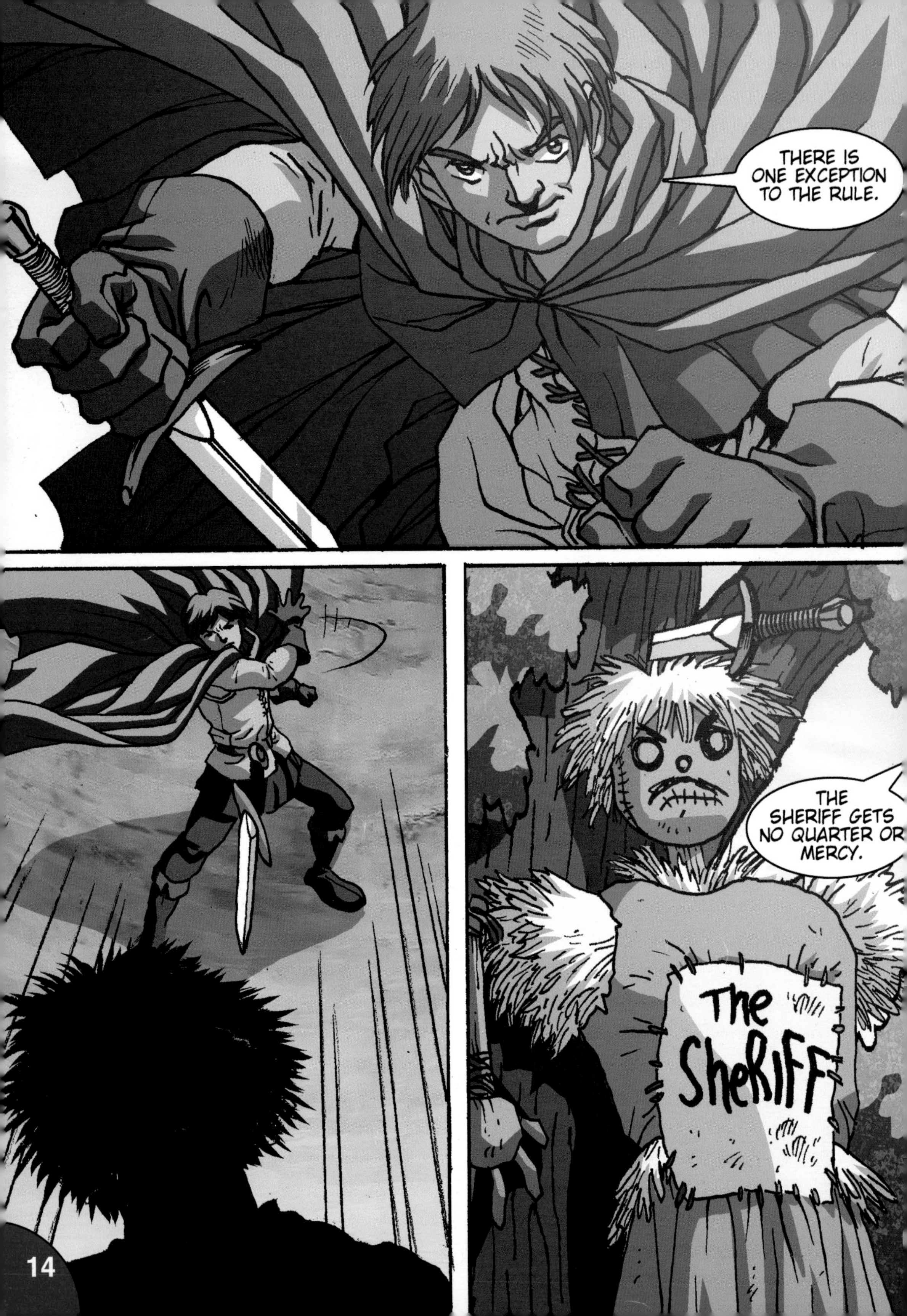
THERE IS ONE EXCEPTION TO THE RULE.
THE SHERIFF GETS NO QUARTER OR MERCY.
The SheRiFF

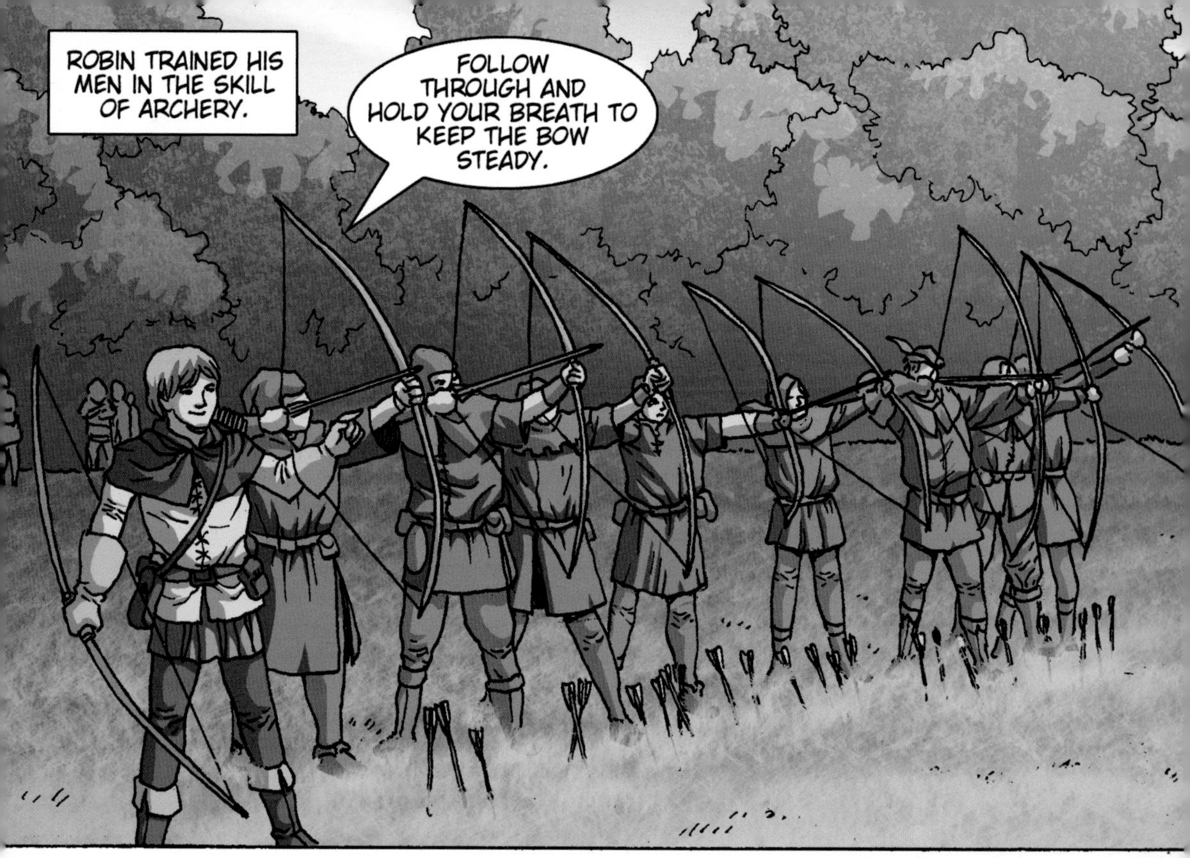
ROBIN TRAINED HIS MEN IN THE SKILL OF ARCHERY.
FOLLOW THROUGH AND HOLD YOUR BREATH TO KEEP THE BOW STEADY.

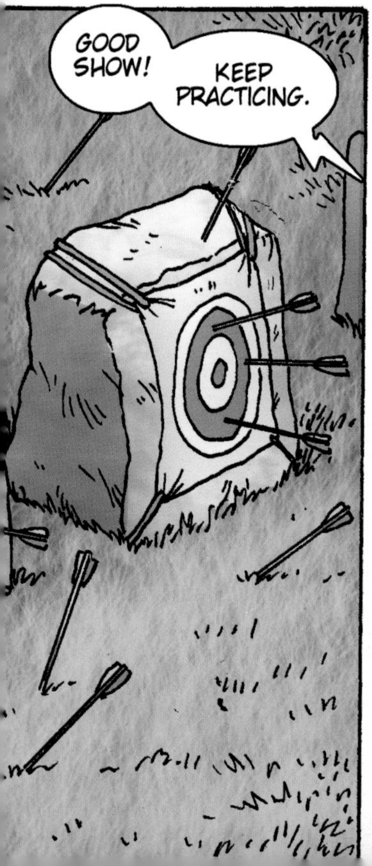
GOOD SHOW!
KEEP PRACTICING.

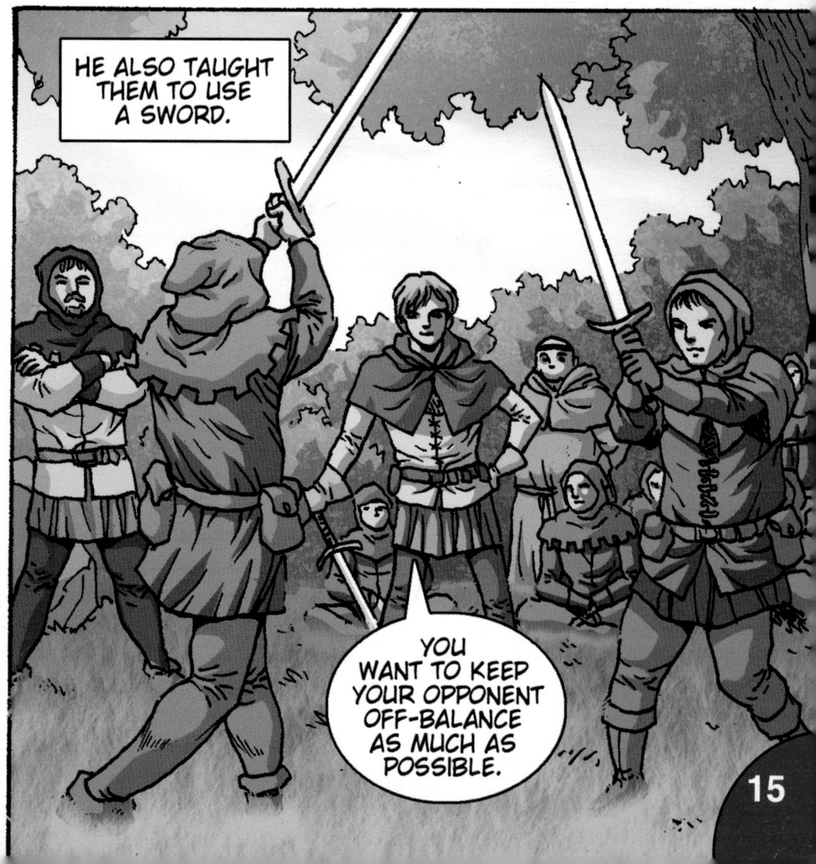
HE ALSO TAUGHT THEM TO USE A SWORD.
YOU WANT TO KEEP YOUR OPPONENT OFF-BALANCE AS MUCH AS POSSIBLE.

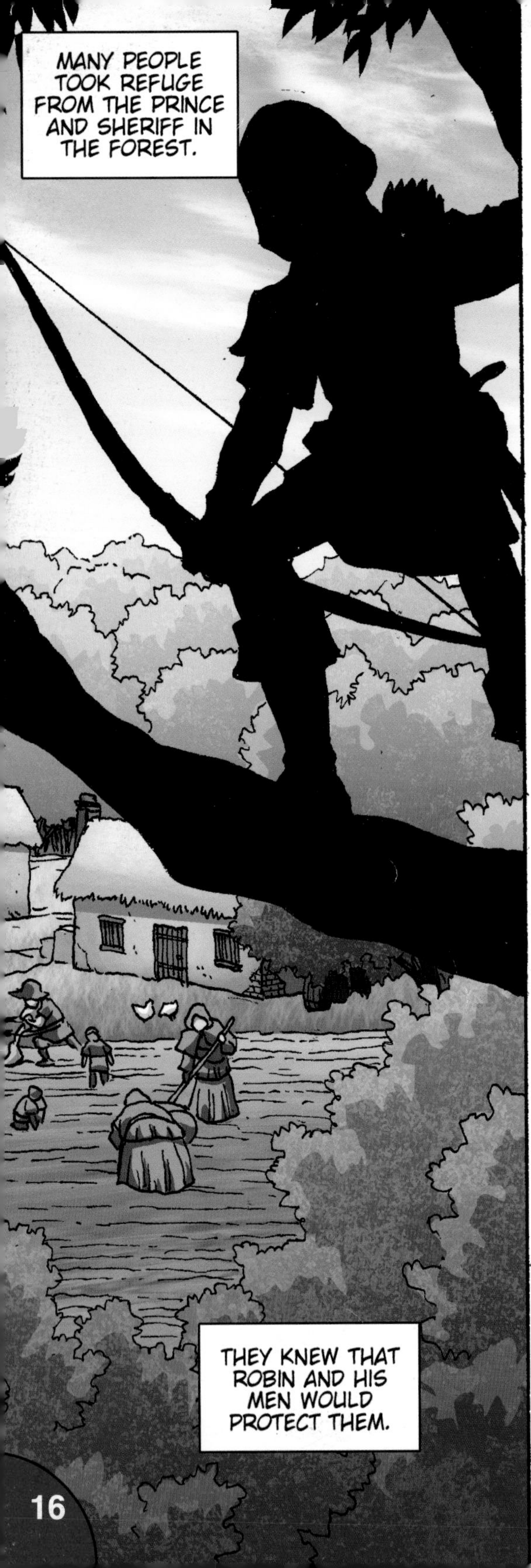
MANY PEOPLE TOOK REFUGE FROM THE PRINCE AND SHERIFF IN THE FOREST.
THEY KNEW THAT ROBIN AND HIS MEN WOULD PROTECT THEM.

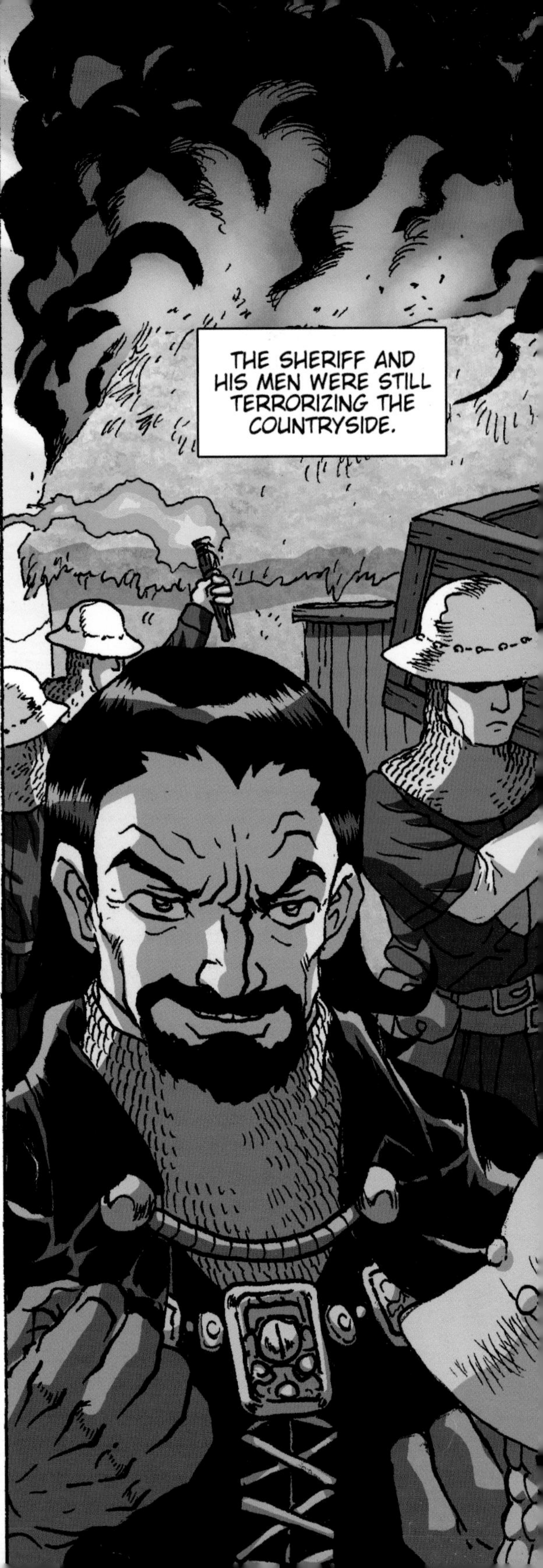
THE SHERIFF AND HIS MEN WERE STILL TERRORIZING THE COUNTRYSIDE.

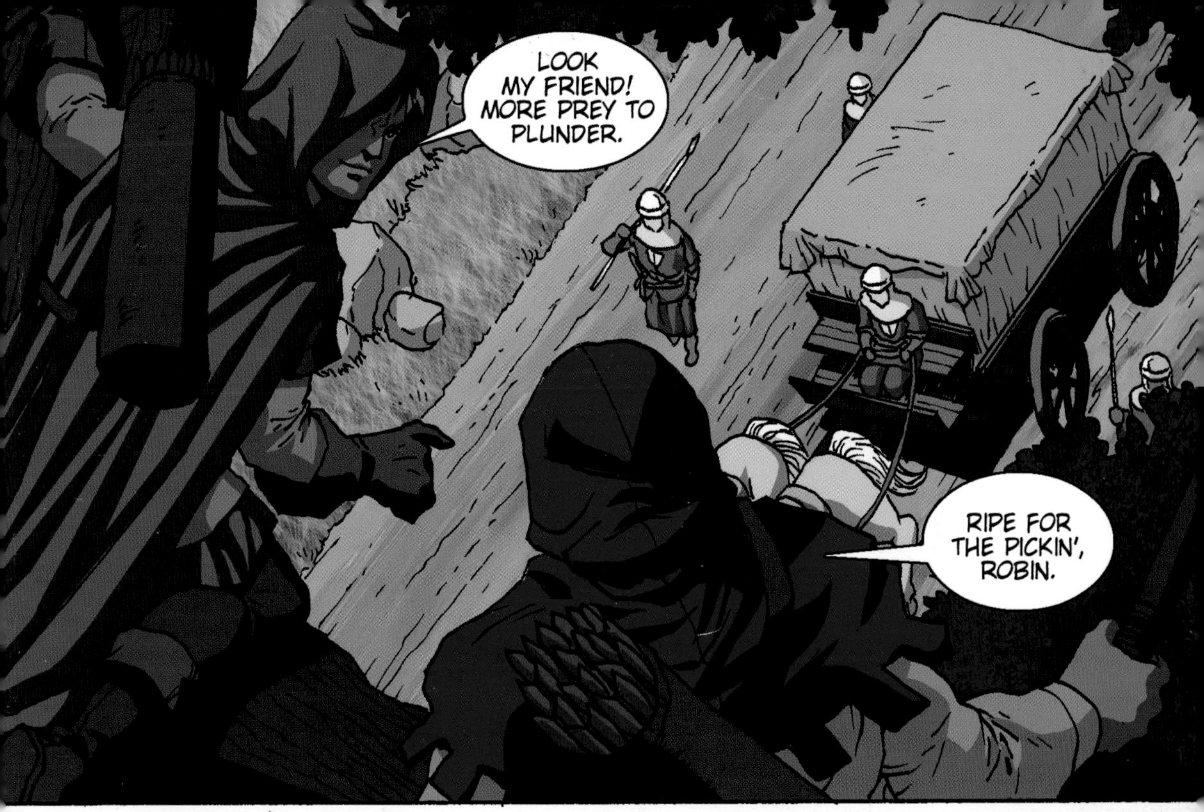
LOOK MY FRIEND! MORE PREY TO PLUNDER.
RIPE FOR THE PICKIN', ROBIN.

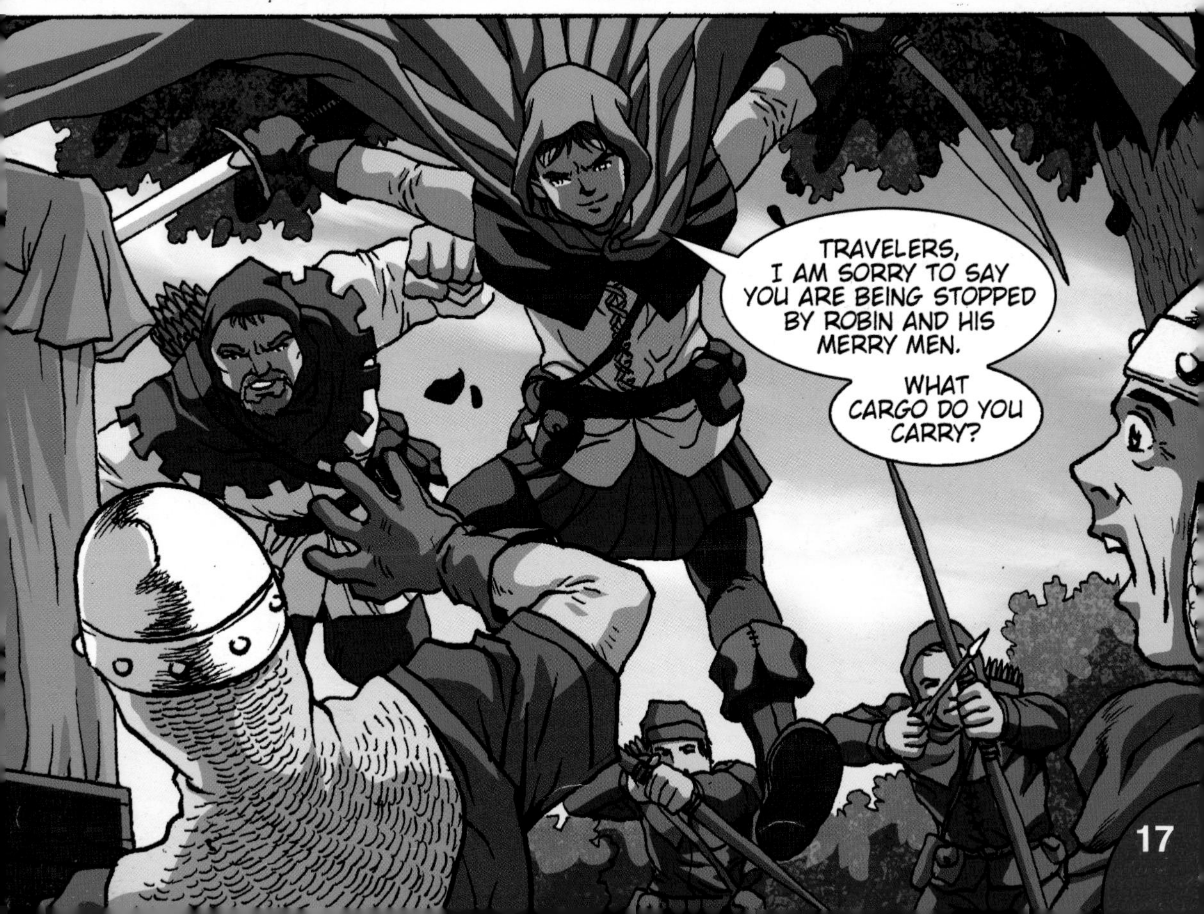
TRAVELERS, I AM SORRY TO SAY YOU ARE BEING STOPPED BY ROBIN AND HIS MERRY MEN.
WHAT CARGO DO YOU CARRY?

Chapter 4 Maid Marian

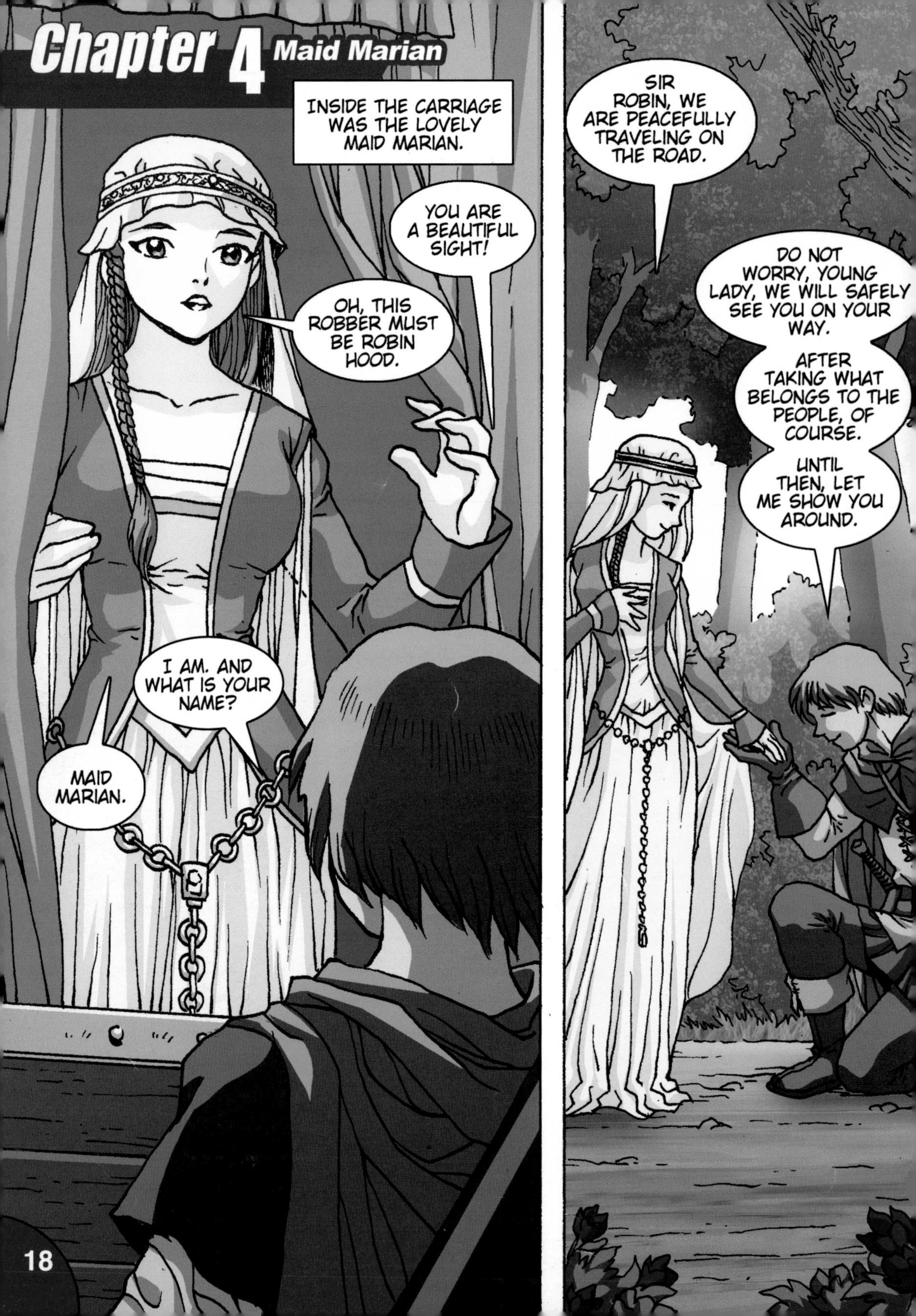
INSIDE THE CARRIAGE WAS THE LOVELY MAID MARIAN.
YOU ARE A BEAUTIFUL SIGHT!
OH, THIS ROBBER MUST BE ROBIN HOOD.
I AM. AND WHAT IS YOUR NAME?
MAID MARIAN.
SIR ROBIN, WE ARE PEACEFULLY TRAVELING ON THE ROAD.
DO NOT WORRY, YOUNG LADY, WE WILL SAFELY SEE YOU ON YOUR WAY.
AFTER TAKING WHAT BELONGS TO THE PEOPLE, OF COURSE.
UNTIL THEN, LET ME SHOW YOU AROUND.

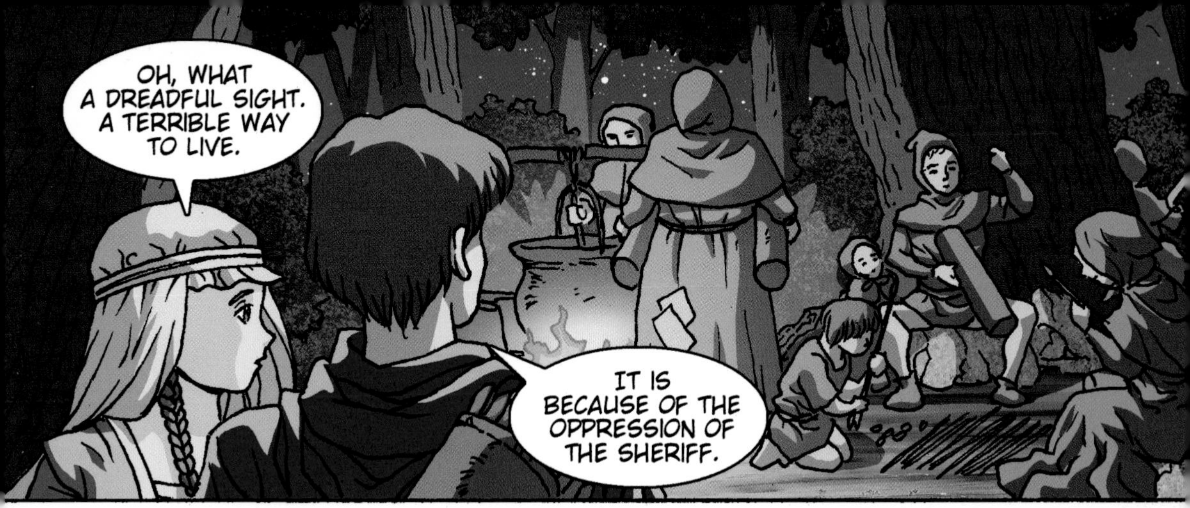
OH, WHAT A DREADFUL SIGHT. A TERRIBLE WAY TO LIVE.
IT IS BECAUSE OF THE OPPRESSION OF THE SHERIFF.

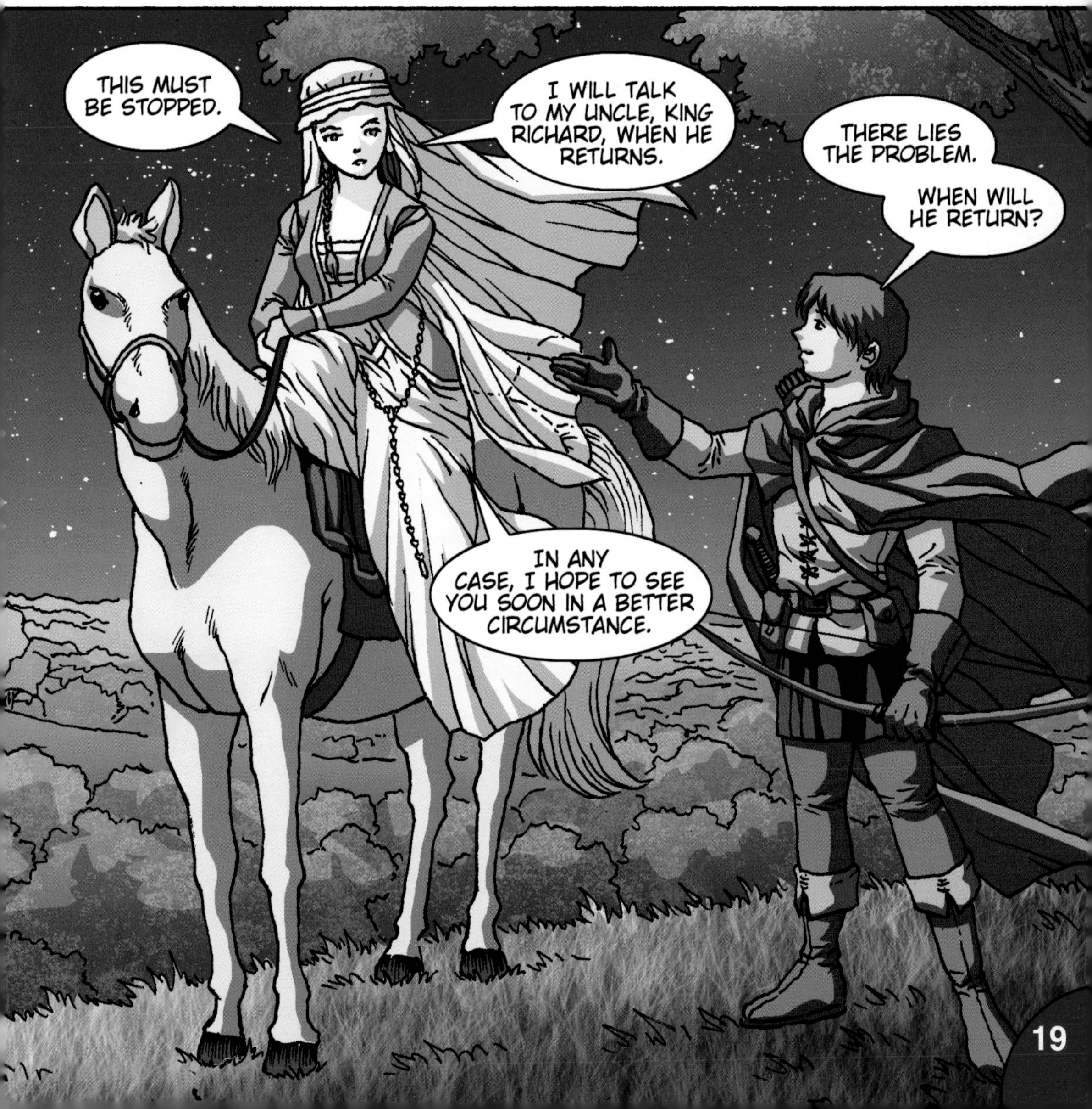
THIS MUST BE STOPPED.
I WILL TALK TO MY UNCLE, KING RICHARD, WHEN HE RETURNS.
THERE LIES THE PROBLEM.
WHEN WILL HE RETURN?
IN ANY CASE, I HOPE TO SEE YOU SOON IN A BETTER CIRCUMSTANCE.

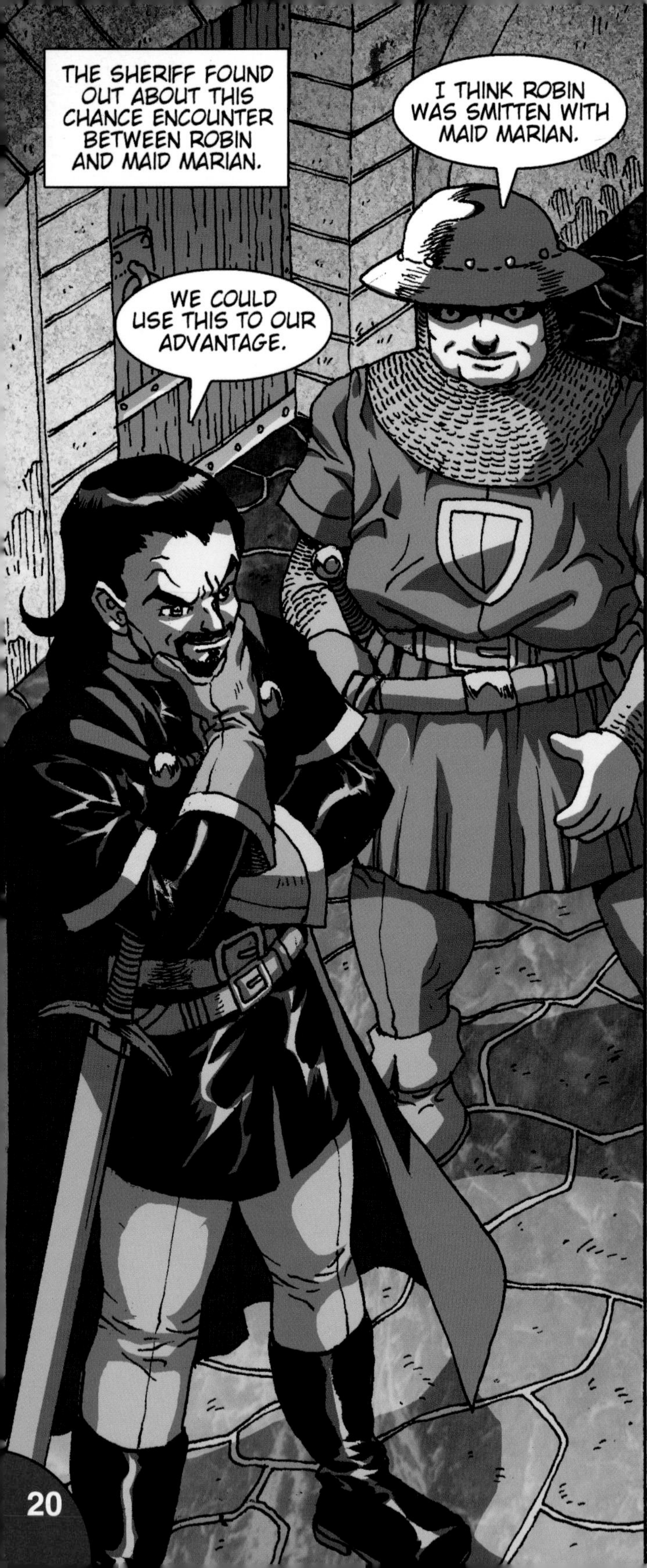
THE SHERIFF FOUND OUT ABOUT THIS CHANCE ENCOUNTER BETWEEN ROBIN AND MAID MARIAN.
I THINK ROBIN WAS SMITTEN WITH MAID MARIAN.
WE COULD USE THIS TO OUR ADVANTAGE.

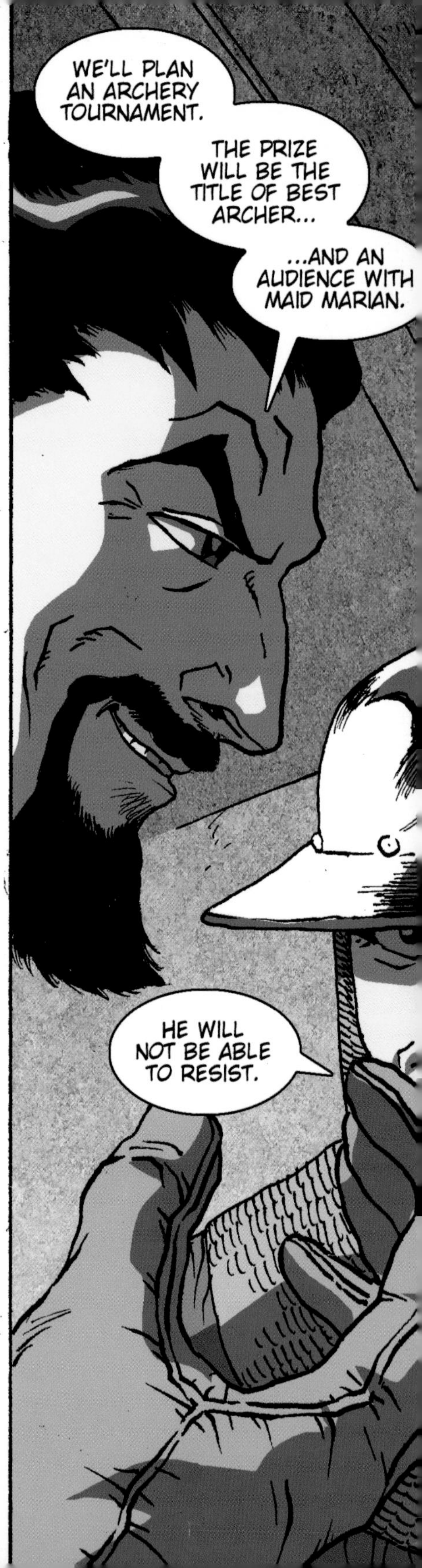
WE'LL PLAN AN ARCHERY TOURNAMENT.
THE PRIZE WILL BE THE TITLE OF BEST ARCHER...
...AND AN AUDIENCE WITH MAID MARIAN.
HE WILL NOT BE ABLE TO RESIST.

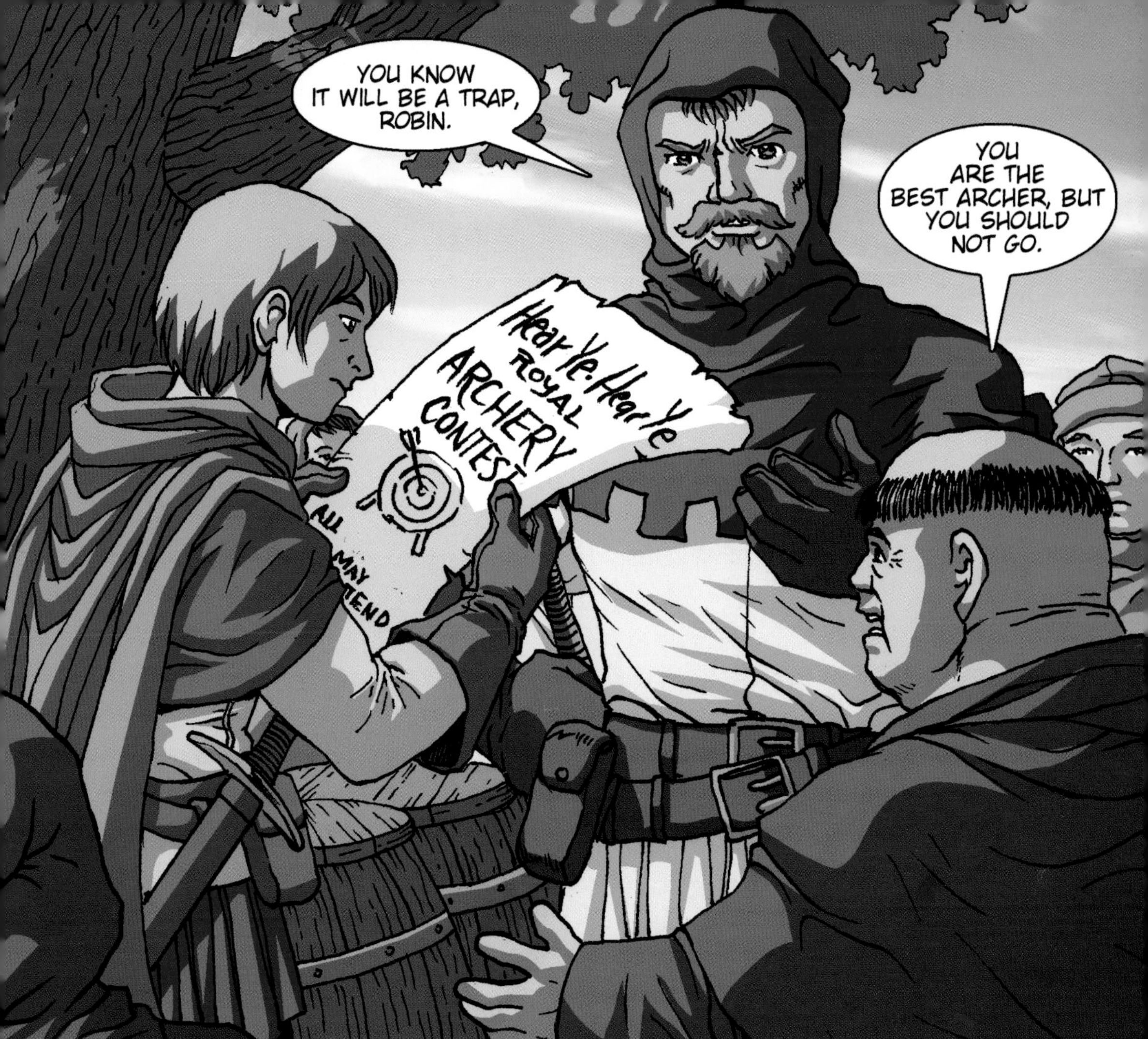
YOU KNOW IT WILL BE A TRAP, ROBIN.
Hear Ye. Hear Ye
ROYAL
ARCHERY
CONTEST
ALL MAY
YOU ARE THE BEST ARCHER, BUT YOU SHOULD NOT GO.

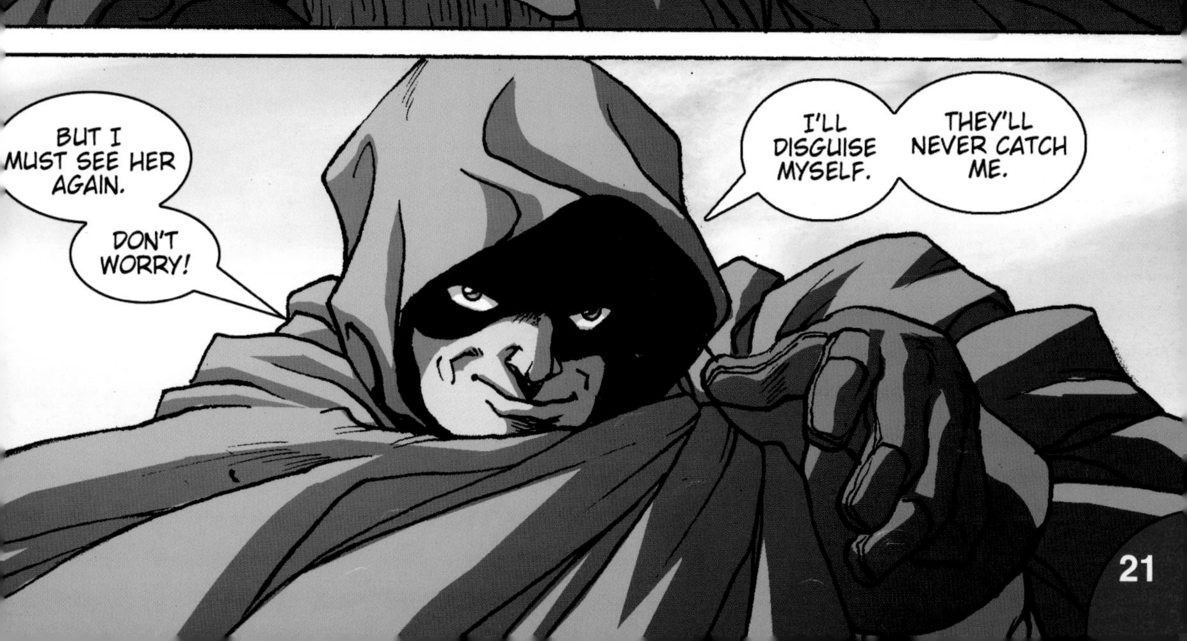
BUT I MUST SEE HER AGAIN.
DON'T WORRY!
I'LL DISGUISE MYSELF.
THEY'LL NEVER CATCH ME.

Chapter 5 The Games Begin

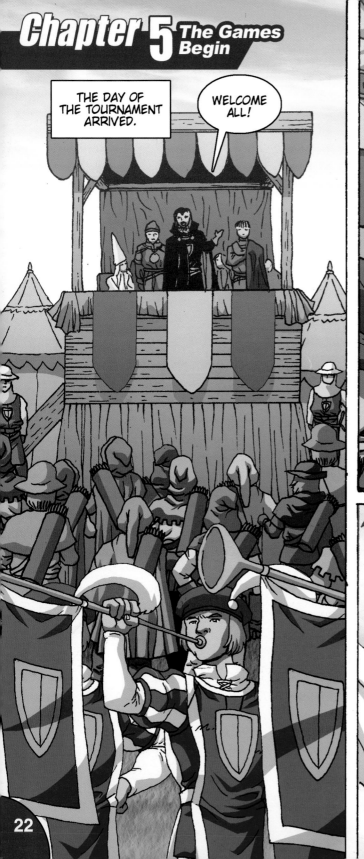

THE DAY OF THE TOURNAMENT ARRIVED.

WELCOME ALL!

THIS DAY WILL DETERMINE WHO IS THE BEST ARCHER OF THE LAND.

LET THE GAMES BEGIN!

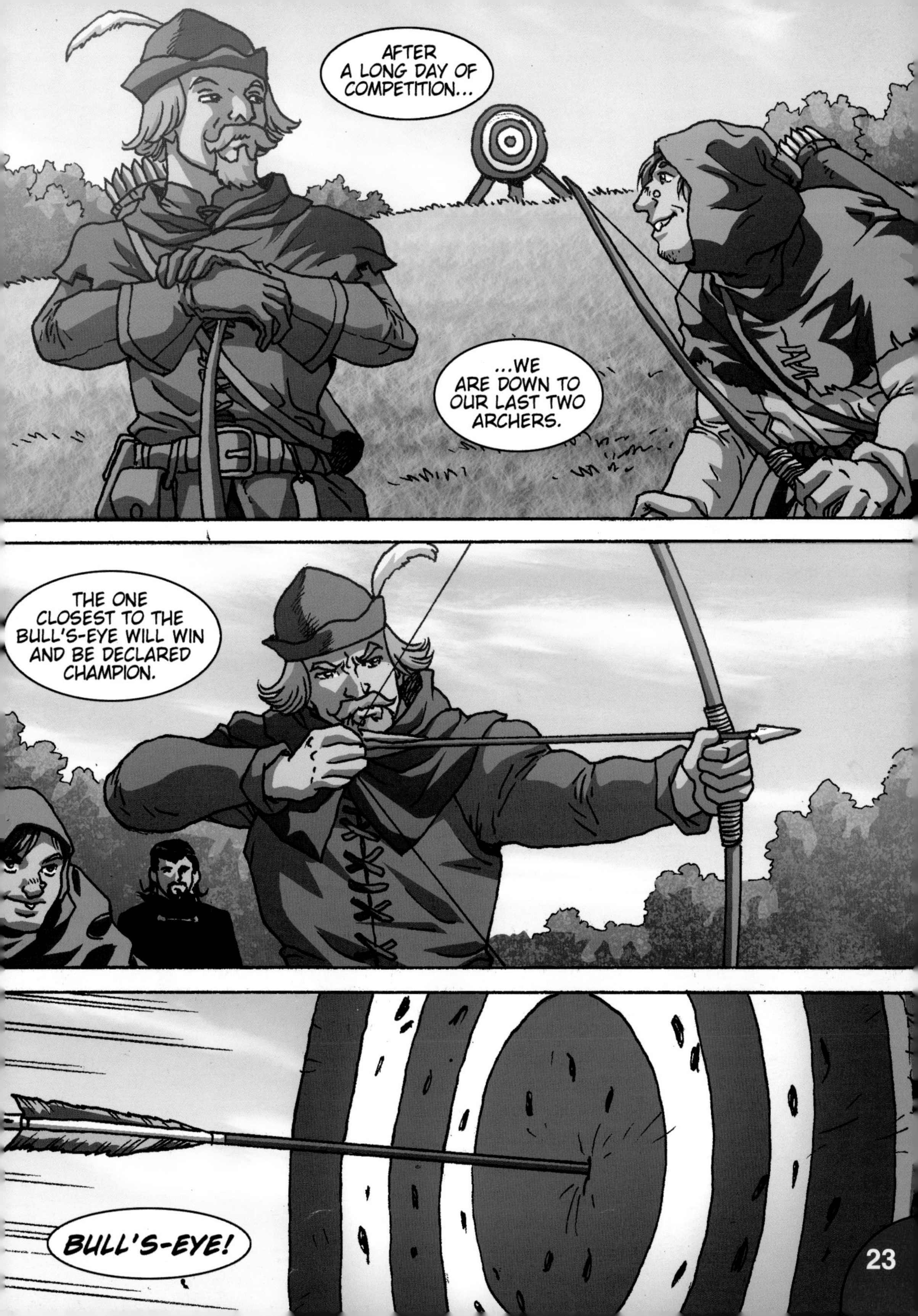
AFTER A LONG DAY OF COMPETITION...
...WE ARE DOWN TO OUR LAST TWO ARCHERS.
THE ONE CLOSEST TO THE BULL'S-EYE WILL WIN AND BE DECLARED CHAMPION.
BULL'S-EYE!

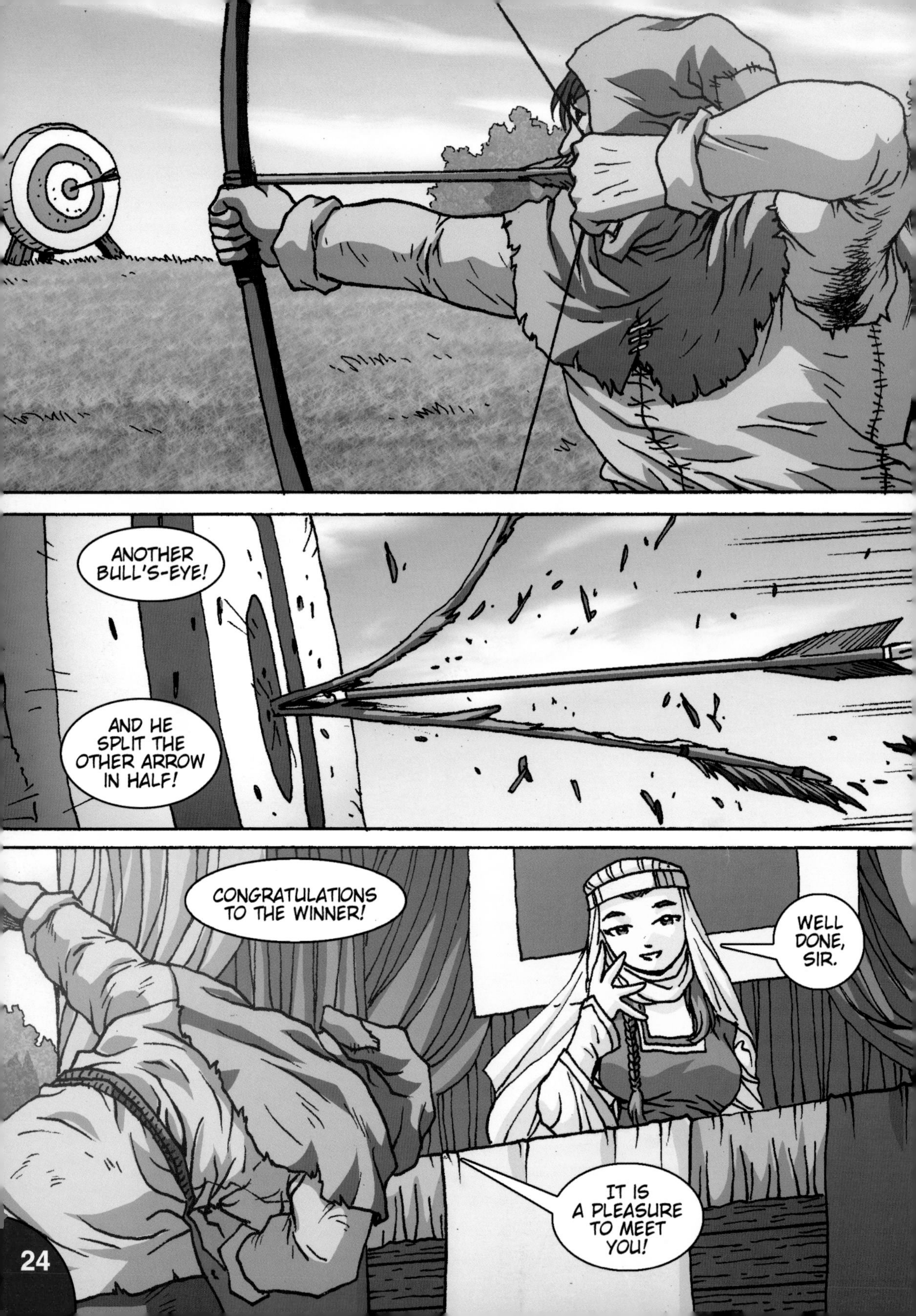
ANOTHER BULL'S-EYE!
AND HE SPLIT THE OTHER ARROW IN HALF!
CONGRATULATIONS TO THE WINNER!
WELL DONE, SIR.
IT IS A PLEASURE TO MEET YOU!

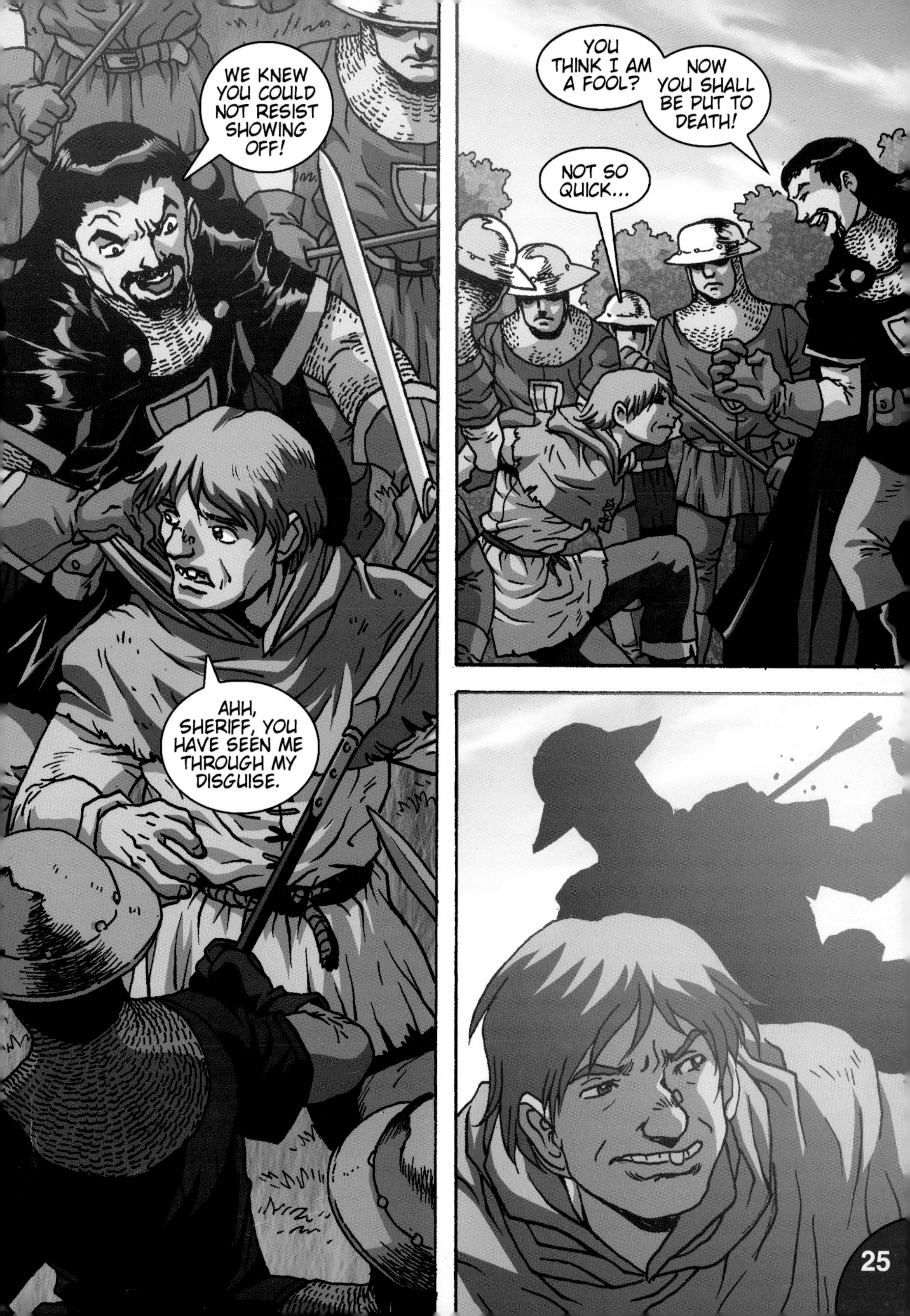
WE KNEW YOU COULD NOT RESIST SHOWING OFF!
AHH, SHERIFF, YOU HAVE SEEN ME THROUGH MY DISGUISE.
YOU THINK I AM A FOOL?
NOW YOU SHALL BE PUT TO DEATH!
NOT SO QUICK...

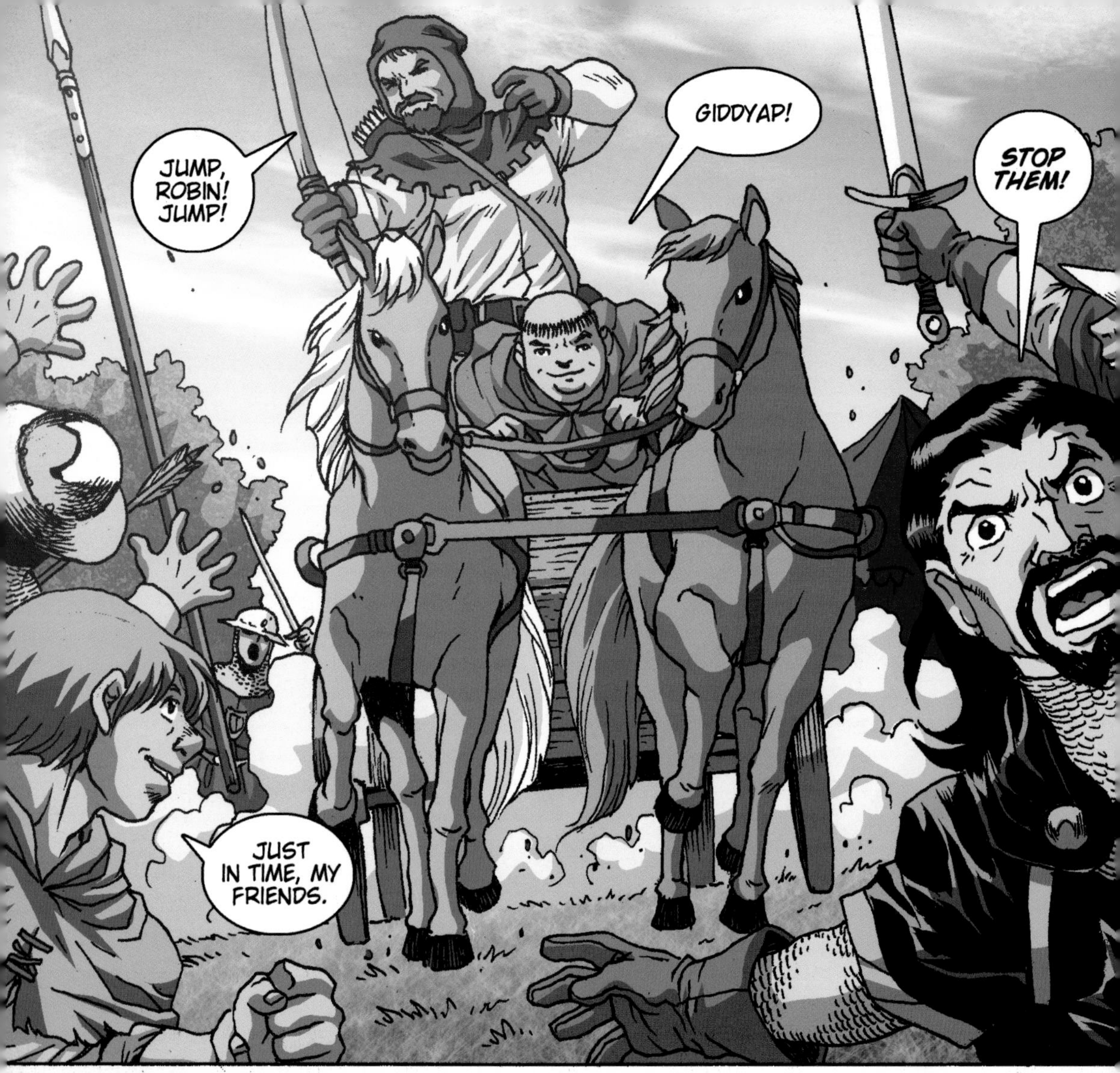
JUMP, ROBIN! JUMP!
GIDDYAP!
STOP THEM!
JUST IN TIME, MY FRIENDS.

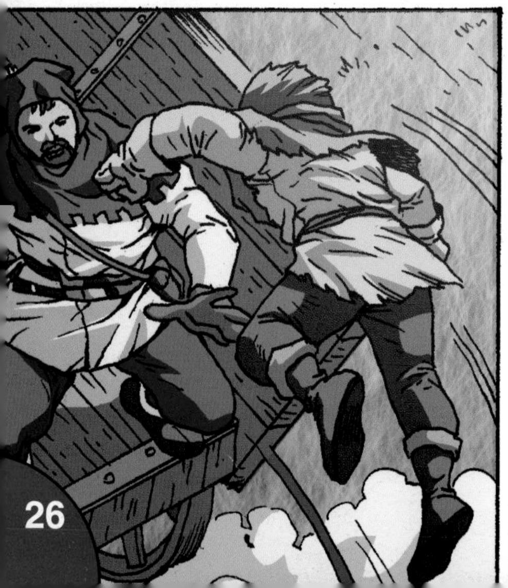

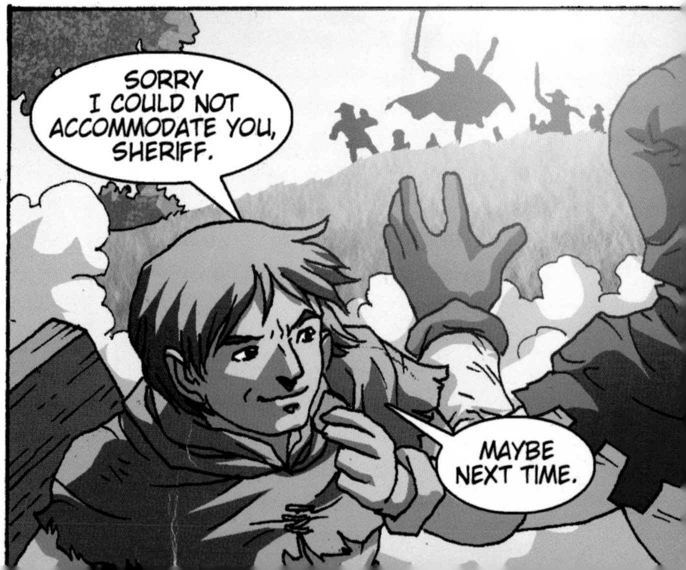
SORRY I COULD NOT ACCOMMODATE YOU, SHERIFF.
MAYBE NEXT TIME.

Chapter 6 The King Returns

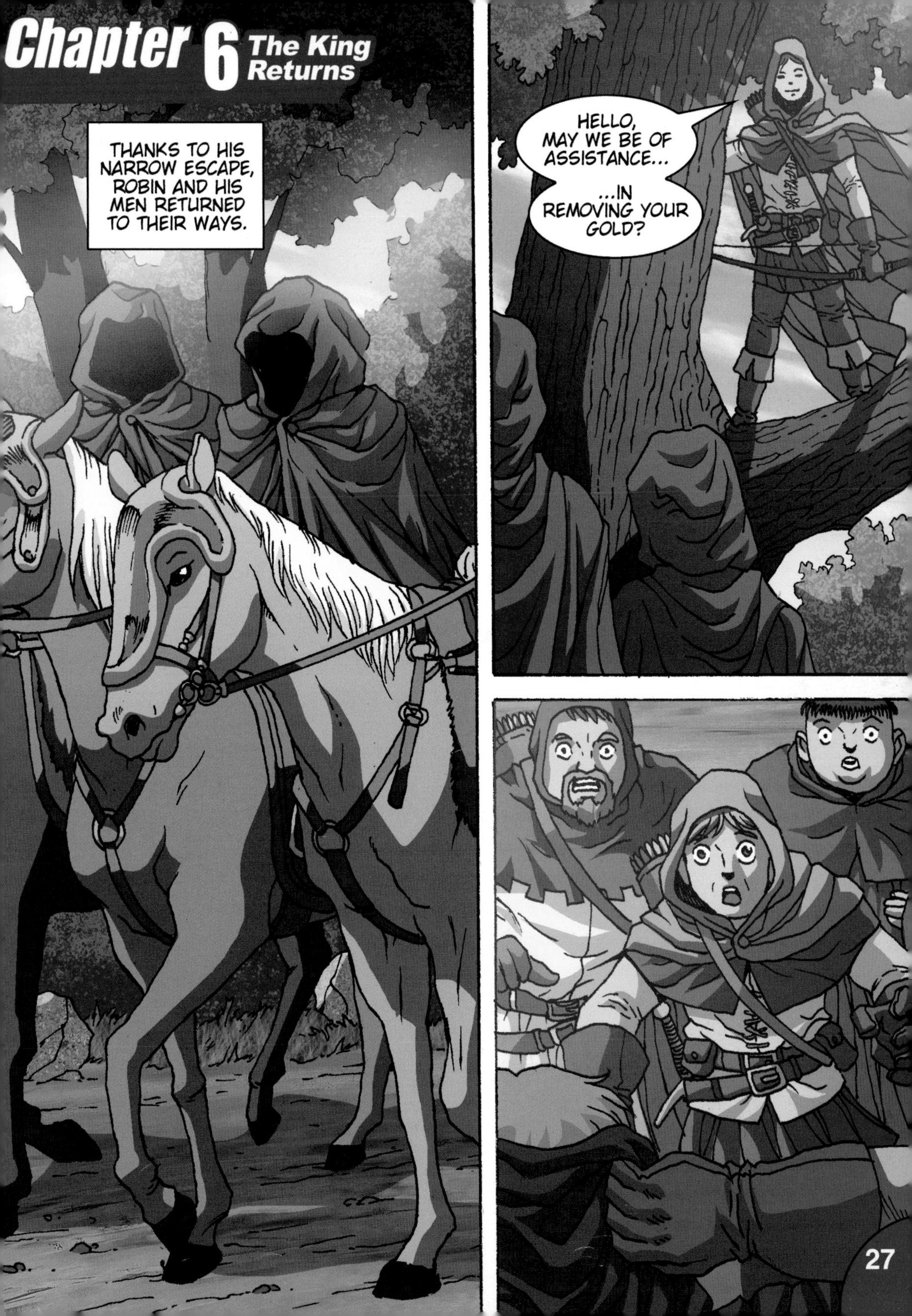
THANKS TO HIS NARROW ESCAPE, ROBIN AND HIS MEN RETURNED TO THEIR WAYS.
HELLO, MAY WE BE OF ASSISTANCE...
...IN REMOVING YOUR GOLD?

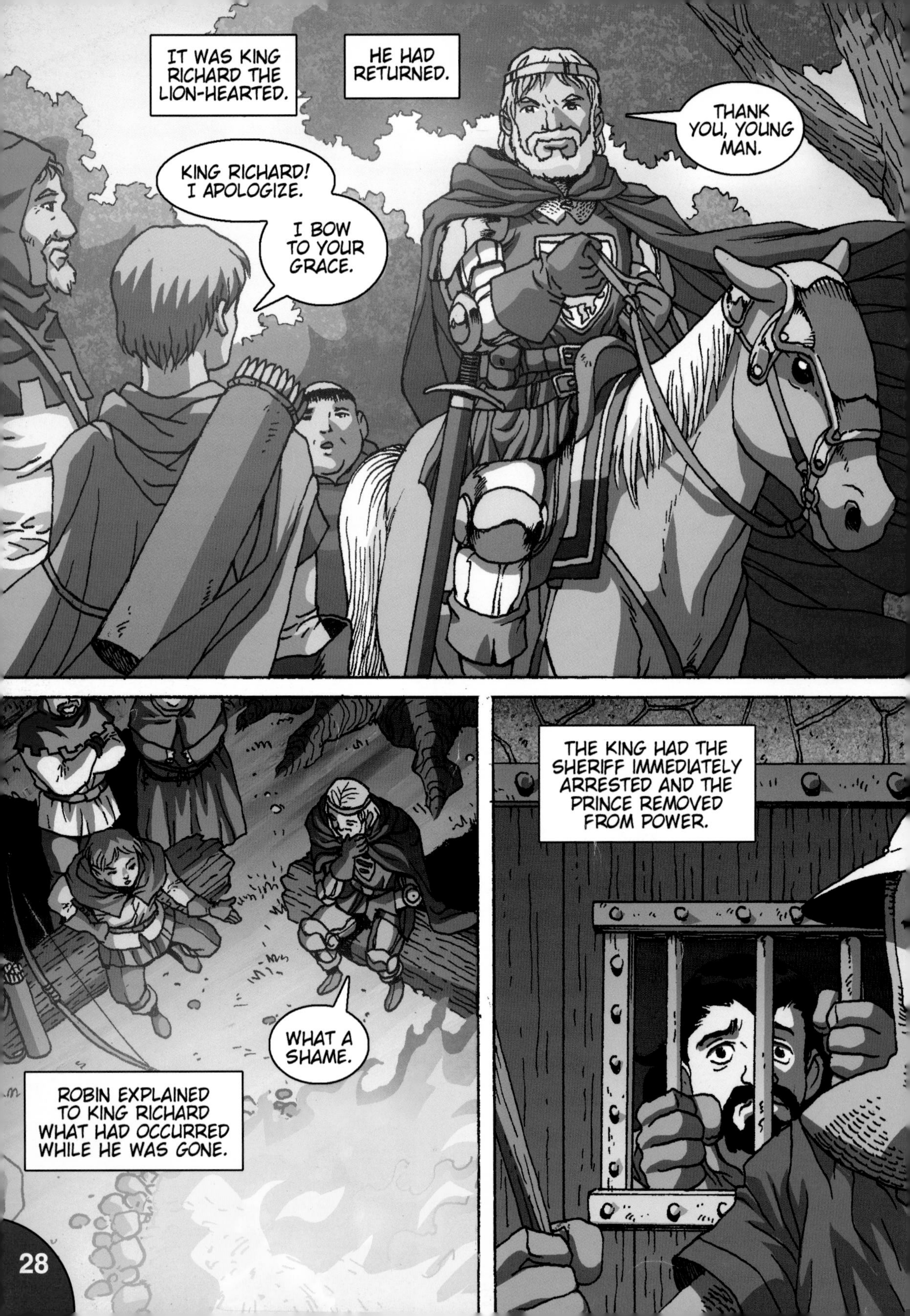
IT WAS KING RICHARD THE LION-HEARTED.
HE HAD RETURNED.
THANK YOU, YOUNG MAN.
KING RICHARD! I APOLOGIZE.
I BOW TO YOUR GRACE.
ROBIN EXPLAINED TO KING RICHARD WHAT HAD OCCURRED WHILE HE WAS GONE.
WHAT A SHAME.
THE KING HAD THE SHERIFF IMMEDIATELY ARRESTED AND THE PRINCE REMOVED FROM POWER.

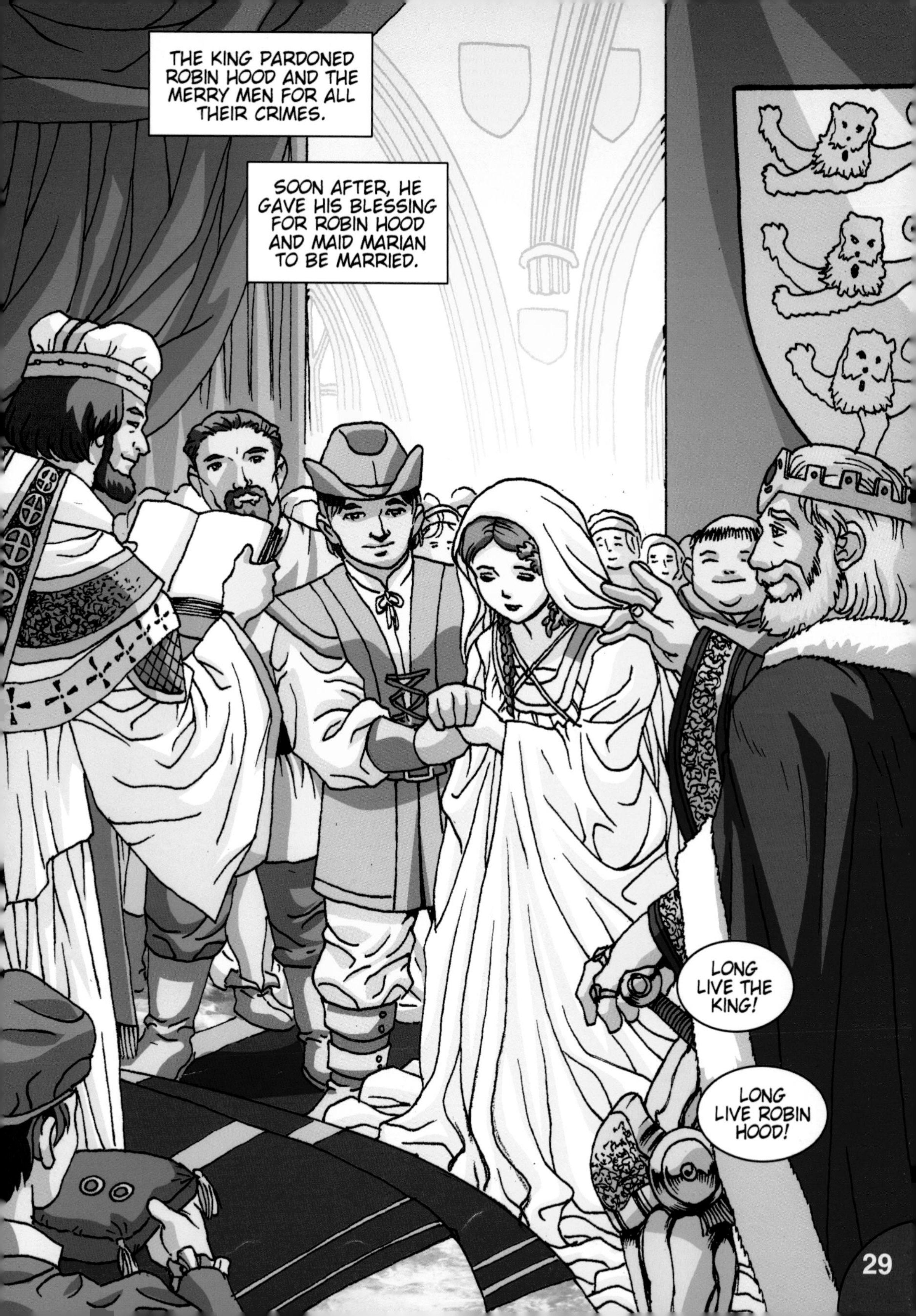
THE KING PARDONED ROBIN HOOD AND THE MERRY MEN FOR ALL THEIR CRIMES.
SOON AFTER, HE GAVE HIS BLESSING FOR ROBIN HOOD AND MAID MARIAN TO BE MARRIED.
LONG LIVE THE KING!
LONG LIVE ROBIN HOOD!

About the Author

Howard Pyle was born on March 5, 1853, in Wilmington, Delaware. He began studying art in his father's leather business. For a time, he studied at the Art Students' League in New York City, too.

In 1876, Pyle became known for his illustrations in books and magazines. He illustrated for *Harper's Monthly* for many years. He also established himself as an illustrator and author of children's stories and fairy tales.

Pyle returned to Wilmington in 1880. There, he established a free art school in his home. Many American illustrators received an education there, including N.C. Wyeth and Maxfield Parrish.

Later, Pyle began painting murals. He was not satisfied with his style. So, he traveled to Italy to continue studying painting. Pyle died on November 9, 1911, in Florence, Italy. He is remembered as one of the most influential illustrators of his time.

Additional Works

Additional Works by Howard Pyle

The Merry Adventures of Robin Hood (1883)
Pepper & Salt (1886)
The Rose of Paradise (1887)
The Wonder Clock (1888)
Otto of the Silver Hand (1888)
Jack Ballister's Fortunes (1895)
The Garden Behind the Moon (1895)
The Ghost of Captain Brand (1896)
The Story of King Arthur and His Knights (1903)

About the Adapter

Joeming Dunn is both a general practice physician and the owner of one of the largest comic companies in Texas, Antarctic Press. A graduate of two Texas schools, Austin College in Sherman and the University of Texas Medical Branch in Galveston, he has currently settled in San Antonio.

Dr. Dunn has written or co-authored texts in both the medical and graphic novel fields. He met his wife, Teresa, in college, and they have two bright and lovely girls, Ashley and Camerin. Ashley has even helped some with his research for these Magic Wagon books.

Glossary

accommodate - to provide with something needed or desired.

Crusades - Christian holy wars fought from the 1000s to 1200s to reclaim the Holy Land from the Muslims.

exploit - a notable or historic act.

oppress - to govern harshly; keep down unjustly or cruelly.

pardon - to forgive anything illegal that a person has done.

serf - a peasant who works the land for the landowner.

stave - a staff used as a weapon.

tariff - the taxes a government puts on imported or exported goods.

Web Sites

To learn more about Howard Pyle, visit ABDO Publishing Company on the World Wide Web at **www.abdopublishing.com.** Web sites about Pyle are featured on our Book Links page. These links are routinely monitored and updated to provide the most current information available.